A WINK AND A NOD

Don Marsh

ISBN-9798683452698

Cover design by: Art Painter
Library of Congress Control Number: 2018675309
Printed in the United States of America

*Dedicated to John D. MacDonald for
introducing me to Travis McGee*

CONTENTS

MCGEE

I have no idea why she called me. I'm not in a place where I would want to start something new. More like being in a place waiting for something old to end. Me.

I'm 80 years old. Everything aches. My hearing's not good. I have a slushy case of edema in my right leg. Possibly a sign of congestive heart failure. And, I have trouble climbing up stairs. I'm only inspired to do so because I can come down the stairs just fine. Carefully but fine. So far.

So, it was living life under these deteriorating conditions that I received a call from a former colleague asking if I could help find out what happened to her husband who disappeared a year ago. She said that after more than 50 years as a journalist, I would probably ask better questions than the cops who had let the case drift into their cold case file. Being tired of falling asleep during afternoon soap operas, old movies and with limited success at crossword puzzles I said I would think about it. What was I thinking?

Was I bored? Was I lonely? Was there a weird synergetic inspiration? I had lost my wife a few years earlier myself. There was no mystery to that one. She was not exactly lost. She left with a liver full of cancer and I knew exactly where she was. In an urn on my bedside table. The questions were easy to answer, and the answer to all of them was yes.

I considered helping because, with encouragement from me, she had rallied to my cause when I abruptly quit my post retirement, part time copy editing job at a neighborhood newspaper. A twenty-something female colleague accused me of disrespecting her for saying she looked pretty. Actually, I had done it two days in a row. Somehow overwhelmed, she complained to management that I had placed a higher value on her appearance than her accomplishments. Truth be told, she wasn't that pretty. I thought I was just being nice. And, her accomplishments were yet to surface.

Management caved. When I realized that male managers were more fearful of her and potential "Me Too" aftershocks, than they were supportive of me, and that "victims" have the juice in cases like this, I told them to "fuck off" and left the building before the discussion had really been called to order. No way I was going to stay in that environment. I put myself out to pasture.

My former colleague, Mary Haller got the story from mutual friends, wrote a supportive letter of complaint to the publisher and posted it online. She introduced me to the 21st century term "snowflake" describing the breed as self obsessed, pathologically needy, hypersensitive, and easily offended.

Jeez. Isn't life tough enough?

Mary's online posting got many "likes" making me a much admired, and a much despised, octogenarian. I sent her a brief thank you note, and put her back in my past. Until that call.

Did I owe her? I never felt I had more than a zero chance of really being able to help. But as I said, I was lonely. I learned quickly that Newton Minow's 50 year old "vast wasteland" of morning, afternoon, and evening television was still valid, not to mention my increasing inability to overcome the frustration of the Times puzzles.

Mary Haller had been an administrative assistant when we still called them secretaries. She worked for my boss at the local television station when I was a so called investigative reporter. I'd had a few scoops dealing with drugs in politics, criminal justice shortcomings and vote fraud. They resulted in some different faces in the same old places.

That didn't mean that my résumé was filled with exposés but rather that I had more time to work on stories than my beat colleagues with their daily deadlines. It also gave me more time to get to know Mary and to tell her when she looked nice without having her freak out. She retired a few years before I did. I attended a small gathering to celebrate the occasion. She said then she was looking forward to spending a lot more time with her husband, doing a little traveling, and, she said with a smile, "finally learning how to cook."

Her husband was there. I had seen him a few times previously at social events. I remembered him as relatively non-descript, quiet, polite, and well muscled after years of lugging glass. He seemed very comfortable letting his wife have the stage. He seemed proud of her. The retirement was a few years ago. Although we had exchanged Christmas cards over those years, we had left each other to our respective lives. Until she called. Out of the blue.

So I put on my jeans, my sneakers, and my most comfortable flannel shirt and made my way to Mary Haller. I thought what I always thought when I left my place. I hoped I wouldn't fall, and was grateful that no one had taken my car away from me. Of course, there was no reason to do that. Unless some busybody started paying attention to the scrape marks on the old Corolla.

She lived in a modest home in a modest neighborhood. Her lawn and shrubs needed attention. When she opened the door, which could have used a coat of paint, her smile made up for any suggestion of faltering upkeep.

Not surprisingly, she looked older than I remembered her which only reminded me that she was undoubtedly thinking the same about me. Except for twinkling blue eyes and a bright smile she was a monochromatic study; gray hair, gray pallor, gray dress. She wrapped her arms around me and gave me a big hug that I returned enthusiastically. "You look wonderful," we both lied simultaneously. With a nod of the head she beckoned me inside to a charming room of comfortable looking eighties' furniture and framed photographs from forever. There was a large floor to ceiling bookcase filled to overflowing. Some books were nestled on the floor. At least one of the two who lived here was a reader.

The room showed no signs of the exterior neglect. I heard a television or radio playing in another room. Despite the overall tidiness, a stream of sunlight punched through a window illuminating tiny particles of something or other floating in the air on their way to table tops, picture frames and waiting lungs.

She brought coffee in china cups about half the size of the hefty mugs I preferred. I had the feeling she was offering her best dainty porcelain and flowered ware. It was flattering. We exchanged the usual pleasantries. So nice to see you. How are you? How have you been? A repeat performance on the fibs about appearance. She offered another cup of coffee. I declined. For a few seconds we sat there in something that might be likened to suspended animation. I with the empty cup giving my hand something to do. She with folded hands in her lap.

I was first to break from the gate. "Now Mary, what's this about your husband?" I asked.

She tightened the grip on her hands. "It's been exactly one year since I last saw him."

"Anniversaries are tough," I said, "Especially hard ones."

"We were married for forty years, lived a good life, had a good marriage." She paused. "And one day he was gone. Poof. He walked out the door one day and didn't come back. Vanished. No word of any kind. No explanation. It's been driving me crazy ever since. The uncertainty. Is he dead? Alive? Murdered? Would he leave me after forty years? If we were half our age I'd assume he left me for someone else. That seems the most unlikely scenario of all now. He was too shy for hanky panky." I could see her eyes cloud with would-be tears. She knuckled them into retreat. She looked at me with an expression that was both puzzled and pleading and needed a response.

"Mary, I'm so sad this has happened to your life," I said. I was uncomfortable. I didn't quite know how to take it from there. Another awkward moment.

"You indicated you thought I might be able to

help. I don't see how. I wish I could. But there was a missing person investigation wasn't there? The cops are much better at this sort of thing than I could ever be. Have you kept in contact...asked them to reopen the case?"

"I have kept in contact ever since. Less and less as the months have gone by. A nice detective calls me from time to time. But he's just being nice and checking on me. I sometimes think he just wants to see if I'm still alive...that if not, he can forget about it all." She looked somewhat embarrassed. "I shouldn't say that. He really seems to just be being friendly."

"Did they have any theories Mary? Anything at all to go on? Any kind of trail, hot cold or otherwise?" She shook her head from side to side.

"Were you getting along?

"We were as much in love when I last saw him as the day we met."

"Any arguments?"

"Nope."

"Was he depressed? Any changes in his personality?"

"Not at all."

I paused, uneasy about my next question.

"Could dementia be part of the story?"

She looked at me incredulously and I understood immediately that that was not a part of the tale. At least not her version. "He was as sharp as the proverbial tack," she said. "As with it as the day we met." She sighed a pathetic sigh. "But that's where the police wanted to go with it. They said the fact that his wallet, cash, driver's license and credit cards were still on the dresser seemed to eliminate concerns about foul play, but left wide open the probability of wandering off. They said it happens a lot.

"Older men and women often hide their fading memories fairly well until one day they leave the house and forget where they live." She shuddered slightly.

"They said that there have been cases where men and women have wandered for miles and are sometimes picked up as John or Jane Does and wind up miles away. Even in other states...in mental institutions. If there's no one to claim them they can stay there a long, long time." Her expression hardened. "One of them even said that those who wander off often wind up at the bottom of a creek or pond. Or the river. My god, when he said that I screamed and kicked him out of the house."

She shook her head from side to side and was wringing her hands. "The nice cop stayed and apologized. He went on to talk about the possibility of foul play, but as time went on that seemed less and less likely to everyone. Again, because of the wallet."

She stopped talking and held my eyes in hers. There was strength in them, and yet a subtle vulnerability too. I think it was at that moment I realized that I would probably try to help although I had no idea how. I took her hands and stroked them gently, noting the liver spots on hers and mine. "Tell me about him and your lives together," I asked.

There were no surprises. She told me they had met after high school and married while she was going to secretarial school and Fred Haller was an apprentice glazier. They never had children though she tried to make a joke about how hard they tried. It didn't work. It was obviously a sad omission from the story.

They did okay financially but were lifetime captives of the middle class. She retired a few years before he did. They did a little traveling, had a small circle of friends but did not socialize much.

He had been a union leader when working, and she heard from his union pals from time to time. He puttered around the house in retirement but only found a hobby to keep him more occupied a few months before he disappeared.

She read and kept house and they were both healthy. Their former employment provided small but adequate pensions, small enough to supplement Social Security rather than the other way around. Medicare was their primary health insurance.

A life insurance policy on Fred was in limbo. Insurance companies, being the beneficent corporate citizens they are, would not honor the policy on Fred without a death certificate or a lengthy period of time in which Fred might be presumed dead. Without a dead Fred, she was in a bind on that front. In this state it might take five to seven years for an insurance check to be written under the circumstances surrounding Fred's disappearance. And probably not without her going to court at that. "I'm not getting any younger," she noted. "Who knows if I'll even be around when they pay off?"

She was getting along but on a tight budget. In short it was the great American saga writ small. But, as is often the case with such stock...no complaints. Until Fred Haller disappeared.

"Mary, what in the world do you think I can do to get to the bottom of Fred's disappearance?" I asked. "I have no expertise for something like this. I'd like to help, but if I thought I could I'd be more enthusiastic. Have you thought about hiring a private detective?"

She shrugged her shoulders. "With what?" she asked. "They cost more than I could manage." She stood and walked to the window to tussle with the Venetian blind. She turned. "I was hoping you could rattle some cages and get the police to get back on it a little more aggressively. I think a man can do that better than a woman." She returned to her seat. "I need to feel that something's being done to bring closure to the matter. God, I hate that word closure, but for the first time I think I get it. If he's alive and out there and confused, I want him back. If he's dead, I want to bury him or give him a marker."

I watched her eyes narrow. The patches of blue disappeared behind two minus signs. And she said with more emotion...more authority than I had heard from her during out entire conversation, "And DAMMIT...I want that insurance money!"

The forcefulness of it took me aback. I was surprised. She saw it.

"Sorry," she said. "As I said earlier, I need closure on this. It's driving me nuts. Not just the insurance. The uncertainty. I really need answers to the questions. Why the hell is he not here with me?" She leaned forward placing her face in cupped hands.

"I don't know," I finally said. "But I also don't know if I'm capable of finding out. Hell, I can hardly walk across the street. How would I walk through all of this?" I didn't say, and probably didn't need to say that insurance companies are willing to settle small claims fast, but not the big ones. I wanted to know the value of the policy, but thinking it really was none of my business, I didn't ask.

Her look softened as if she understood my dilemma. She said nothing as we sat trying to avoid each other's eyes. There was a long silence as we each retreated to our own thoughts.

After a few moments she asked, "Did they ever apologize to you?"

"What?" I was surprised at the sudden shift in topics.

"Apologize for cutting you loose at the paper."

"Hah. Where did that come from? That's old news Mary. Thanks again for your support on that." I thought back on my life's most recent drama.

"No. No apology. These are different times. Victimhood wins. There's a young generation of would be 'Me Too' warriors just waiting for a perceived offense. If a young women says I disrespected her or womanhood in general, I can't win. There's no defense for it."

I sensed she was reminding me that she had come to my side supporting me in a time of stress. Was she leaving me any other choice but to come to hers?

"You got screwed."

"No," I said. "I just got old. Ageism. A Millennial hit job." I thought about it for another moment. I was still hurt by the way I had been jettisoned, even though I cut myself loose. No one was begging me to stay. "No big deal. I miss having someplace to go and having something to do, but there was no money in the gig at the paper. It was more of a place to go everyday."

I thought more about it for a moment. "There's been a lot written about it lately. Interestingly, a lot of the new literature on it is written by women. They call it 'victim feminism'...'privileging of victimhood'... 'pathological vulnerability.' It's all part of a 'call out culture.' Hard to defend against. Go with it, or just go as a result of it. I'm too old to fight it. As I say, It's old news."

She thought about it for a moment. "It's generational, that's a big part of it. But I'm sure you understand that young women...all women...have more than a little reason to feel like it's time to stand up. They...we...have been victimized and marginalized for a long time. But, that being said, a lot of younger women today do seem to be on the warpath. Mad as hell and not going to take it anymore kind of thing."

"Hey, I get that. I've mentored dozens of young women over the years. But, it's hard to accept this generation growing up with the helicopter parent...everybody gets a trophy...the 'I'm entitled' state of mind."

"Have you heard the latest?" she asked slipping away from this part of the discussion. "They say 'Go Boomer' if you say anything they consider out of touch with the times."

"Hah. Well, I'm not a Boomer by almost ten years. "I prefer to call myself a member of the 'Greatest Generation" although I'm somewhere in between. I'm of the Silent Generation. I'm living up to that moniker. I could be the poster child."

"Did you know that the "assassins" are all

gone?" she asked changing direction. "The "pretty young thing's gone on to teach square dancing in the inner city. Can you imagine that? I understand she's writing a book on Emily Dickinson." She rolled her eyes.

"Jesus."

"Her enabler has skipped a couple of rungs on the corporate ladder and is now at least one rung beyond his capacity."

"He always was," I said. "I believe in Karma."

"Good luck with that."

"How do you know all this stuff?" I asked.

She did a pretty version of a Mona Lisa smile and cocked her head and wagged her finger in a way that made her look like a child saying, "I'll never tell."

I could only imagine her sources. But unlike me, she no doubt maintained some contact with former colleagues.

We talked about the old days in old newsrooms. They were days in which gallows humor prevailed and women didn't. Of course, they were barely present. When they were, it was behind the scenes unless they were bringing coffee. And when a few emerged to report, they didn't even get the courtesy of bylines when doing five hundred words on the latest garden club meeting. It wasn't fair, but it was the way it was.

Political correctness was an unknown concept. Black humor prevailed when sardonic wasn't good enough. I recalled a typed memo on the newsroom door. Half in jest, it was still an unofficial edict, in which the death of one American was worth two Brits, three Frenchmen, four Germans, sixteen Bolivians and seventeen thousand Pakistanis and so on. Funny at the time. But editors more or less followed the yardstick back in the day. It seemed the right day for that sort of thing then and is clearly the wrong day now. As we recounted those "good old days" it made us both cringe.

But, there are, it seems to me, other journalistic weak spots that only provide audiences with more anesthesia for their critical thinking skills. Mesmerized by their seventy two inch screens and fast food commercials, audiences seem completely content to watch myriad channels that force feed them "news" that meets their preconceived notions of the world. Or they're content to be euthanized by the other pap that shows them who sings or dances best, or who comes up with the new sitcom format which always seems strikingly familiar. I told her that I was considering a new hobby...whittling while not watching television.

She told me that she had turned to NPR until she realized she had something more important on her mind than listening to the songs of whales. Especially since the death of Cokie Roberts, and since Diane Rehm had left to promote death with dignity, Then replaced by a Rap apostle.

"We're old and jaded," I suggested.

"We're old and pissed," she responded.

"No," I said. "We're just old."

"I prefer elderly." She looked tired.

I looked at her. Poor thing I thought. I'll see what I can do. Poor me.

I told her I was "in." She kissed me dryly on the cheek. "Thanks," she said simply giving me a hug. I stood, with difficulty. The back, the legs the shoulder protesting the intrusion on their quiescence.

"What's the name of the cop?" I asked. "The nice one."

"Detective Paul Ansini," she responded. "I'll get you his number." It was a not so subtle suggestion that I get right on it.

Number in hand, I left pondering whether my decision came as more of a surprise to her, or to me? And then wondering yet again what the hell had I finally decided to take on?

I had trouble tracking down Ansini. He was not in his office. Out on a case I was told. What kind of a case was not disclosed. It could have been a homicide, carjacking, domestic abuse, or a cat in a tree as far as I knew. Cops are like journalists. They get up and go to work usually with no idea as to where the day's work would take them. I left a message with my cell phone number and went on a few errands.

I made it a point to take my phone with me. I was still not used to the digital world. Nomophobia had not infected me yet. Most of the time I forgot the cell. It was usually of no consequence. I rarely received calls, and even more rarely made them. It seemed that my relationship with the phone pretty much consisted of charging the battery and wondering why I was spending so much money for it every month. But, my friends all had them and laughed at me for a long time before I became one of the digital lemmings and signed a long term plan. They had convinced me that there was so much I could do with the phones. Apps. They loved to talk about apps. Pictures. They reveled in showing me photos of the grandkids. Their phones were galleries the rivaled the Louvre. I don't believe, however, there were many pictures of kids with runny noses inside that particular Parisian landmark. Now that I was one of them, it was more difficult for me to criticize those who carried cells constantly and used them frequently for myriad purposes other than actually making phone calls. I was hearing more and more stories of people walking into traffic while texting, or bumping into lamp posts while walking down Main Street checking email.

The call from Ansini came while I was at the grocers trying to figure out what I could get that would require the least amount of time or culinary talent to prepare. My cell does not have a standard ring. When a call comes in, the ringtone is actually he sound of a barking dog. I figured it was better than actually having a dog. No walks in the rain. No poop to clean up. No fleas. They began barking when I was in the checkout line, much to the amusement of the others around me. "I have a dog in my pocket" I explained as I stepped aside to take the call.

Paul Ansini did not sound like a man with a lot of patience. When I helloed he got right to the point. "Detective Paul Ansini here. What do you want?"

I was tempted to say "Hey, you called me," but he didn't sound like a guy with a sense of humor either. I got right to the point.

"Detective Ansini...my name is McGee...Tom McGee. I'd like to talk to you about the disappearance of Fred Haller."

Silence. Then, "Haller? He's been AWOL for more than a year. Do you have any information about him?"

"No, but I'm a friend of his wife..."

"Nice lady" he interrupted.

"Yes she is. Could you give me a couple of minutes at your office in the next day or two? I'd like to talk about the case with you."

His response was anything but enthusiastic, so I had to resort to some bullshit. I told him I was not only a friend to Mary Haller, but also a freelance writer who had promised her I'd do a story on the disappearance. I explained that she was hopeful it would jostle some memories somewhere. I suggested it might be helpful to him in breathing new life into the investigation.

"There is no life in that investigation to breathe new life into," he said with what sounded like certain rejection. I pulled out a card I had played before in another life.

"I'd like to stop by for a few minutes...get a few shots of you, ask a couple of questions then get out of your hair. I know you've probably got a lot on your plate."

"Huh...ya think?

There was an awkward silence. I thought he had hung up.

"Five minutes. My office downtown. Nine sharp. Five minutes! Don't be late." Click. End of connection.

The conversation promised to be interesting. Not lengthy obviously, but interesting in terms of form rather than substance, of which I expected very little. But, a promise is a promise.

The next step was for me to pay for the eggs and cereal, then get home to practice with my cell camera. I had never used it. But I think that's what did the trick. We all have at least a little ego, including gruff police detectives not opposed to appearing full frontal so to speak in a slick magazine. I also had to come up with a snappy name for my fictitious publication. That would pretty much take up the rest of my afternoon. At least it was something to do.

I arrived at the appointed place at the appointed time and was ushered in with no ceremony.

"Didn't you used to be on television?" I was surprised. It had been a long time since my television days. I was a lot older and didn't think I looked anything like the reporter I once was. But from time to time I was recognized by old timers. Every once in a while someone would say, "I grew up watching you." Believe me, as you get older, it is not necessarily flattering to have someone beyond middle age saying they watched you as a kid.

"You've got a good memory," I said. "It's been a lot of years."

"I grew up watching you," he said. I took a deep breath.

"I remember a story you did on the mayor's press secretary selling pot from the basement at city hall. Did you know that he applied to become a cop after he was released?"

"No. I hope he wasn't hired." Ansini laughed in a way that sounded a little like a laugh and a lot like a growl.

Paul Ansini was either the prototype police officer or Mafia consigliere. He was swarthy, beefy and fiftyish. Don Corleone redux. The picture would have been complete if he'd been cleaning his fingernails with a stiletto.

His face was puffy indicating fondness for

booze and pasta. His eyes matched his thick black hair which was combed straight back a la Al Pacino. It could have been a dye job, but somehow he didn't appear the type, although there seemed to be an ego there I thought, as I reminded myself that he hopped on my request for a meeting only after my promise of a published photograph and a little publicity.

He seemed confident, as many cops are, and I thought it was likely he operated on a short fuse but by the book. I would be in trouble I thought if he learned my cover was bogus.

He was dressed in a suit that was dark and lumpy, and a week or two beyond a needed trip to the dry cleaners. His tie stopped well above his belt and rode like a living thing on an ample belly that was wrapped in a white on white shirt. His office was small and that probably made him look bigger than he appeared to be.

"McGee right? What paper are you with?" As an afterthought, "Where's your photographer?" I held up my cell phone. "I'm it," I said

"It's Tom McGee. But people call me Trav."

"Why?"

"I was a big fan of the John D. MacDonald character in his Travis McGee books back in the day. Folks started calling me 'Trav' and it stuck."

He looked disappointed. I don't know if it was my name, or the lack of one for my fictitious publication.

"Was he a cop?"

"McGee? Nope. MacDonald's a helluva writer. Better than average. He put McGee in tricky situations with some pretty slick results. "

"So you think you're this...Travis McGee?"

"Nope. He lived on a boat in Florida. I live in a condo here. I'm just helping a friend whose world turned upside down a year ago."

"I know the lady." He added quickly, "She's no shrinking violet. She kicked my partner out of the house like he was soccer ball."

I pulled out a pad to burnish the phony reporter persona. He nodded. He understood this was on the record. He'd obviously done this dance before.

"He was out of line," he continued. "Not because of what he said but because of the way he said it." He scratched his chin and squinted as if this has been difficult for him to admit.

"This is not a 'tricky situation," he went on. "This is about an old guy who went out to buy the proverbial pack of cigarettes, or whatever, and never came back. Best bet, he got lost on a fuzzy walk and is funny putty and bones in the woods someplace or in the river. Longshot...he forgot his name, address, phone number and wife, and is John Doe someplace outstate or out of state dead or alive." He tapped the fingers of both hands together in what I had once been told was a power gesture. "And...let's face it. Maybe he just got tired of the old lady." He looked at me hard. "Clean up my language on that will you?" He was thinking about my "article."

"So how much of that have you been able to un-scramble in your investigation?"

"We've gone as far as we can go until someone gives us something to go on. His name, rank, ser-ial number and picture have been distributed to law enforcement and hospitals all over the coun-try. Nada. Nix. My guess is he's dead someplace."

"Thinking foul play at all?"

"Nah. If he'd been robbed or mugged and killed we'd know. We'd have a body by now."

"Unless," I suggested, "someone hid the body."

"Street criminals don't work that way. He had left his money at home. If a thug tried to roust him and got nothing for his trouble. He might blow him away, but not take the trouble to bury him someplace."

"What about enemies? Any indication anyone didn't like him. He owed them money? He was a bad neighbor? An asshole?"

"Nothing like this that we could find." He went back to the finger tapping, jabbing one finger onto the desktop for emphasis. "Look McGee. There are thousands of cases like this all over the country every year. We can't do more than we can do. We investigate, get the word out, hope for a break, but have to move on. It's a tough world out there and we're busy enough as it is." He shook his head in a way that communicated too bad... that's the way it is. He didn't need to say it.

"I get it with the wife. I know she's crushed. I talk to her from time to time unless she's out of town. But I can't give her a thing to help her through this. If someone comes forward, we'll be on it like white on rice. But until that happens, like I say, nada."

I nodded. I understood. I had felt the same way the first moments I talked with Mary. "She appreciates those calls," I said. "They help in their own way."

"Thanks," he said standing, a clear indication that my five minutes were up. Actually, it had been fifteen. I left with a much different impression of Ansini than I had expected after that first phone contact. I decided I liked the guy. He was what he was, like so many cops I had come to know over the years, a stereotypical cop who was probably overworked, underpaid, and underappreciated by the people he served, and perhaps even by some he served with. I wasn't so sure his feeling about me might be reciprocal. I hoped it was. We all love being loved.

He never asked the name of my phony publication. And, I never took his picture. But the bottom line remained. Just as I thought, I came away from Ansini with nothing more than I had gone in with.

I clunked back to my place in my aging Corolla

not sure what to do next or if there was going to be a next? If it was a dead end at the beginning where could it go from here? Not the stuff of inspiration. Not the way to get energized. Maybe I'd better have another talk with Mary. What was there to say other than to reinforce the futility of my involvement? After the talk with Ansini I felt even less invested in trying to get answers for Mary than I had at the beginning.

I parked my car, went inside, and poured a hefty glass of Boodles Gin over a small mountain of ice. It was my homage to Travis McGee. I had followed his lead. He was a Plymouth Gin drinker in the early days. When the British distillery was bought out by an American competitor, McGee went to Boodles preferring the British version. I did too. It was my only extravagance, and my source of reinforcement before contacting Mary. I called. She was out. I was glad.

Mary's place was close enough to walk to and if I were a younger man, I would not have hesitated. Out of the question today. And, there was always that fear of falling. My exercise regimen pretty much consisted of shuffling to my car and back. My back hurt all the time and it cut down on my walking. I tried a stationary bike at a local gym, but it cost more each month than a bottle of Boodles and it was boring. And, it didn't help.

I tried her again the next morning. She seemed excited to hear from me. I suppose she thought I might have news of a miracle. Her excitement faded quickly when I said I knew nothing more than I did when we last talked. She asked me to come by. I said I'd be there in an hour. I was and was surprised to see her mowing the lawn. I'd have offered to help but was put off by the fear she would accept. With this back I could no more handle a lawn mower than I could wrestle an alligator. She saw me get out of the car and raised her hand signaling that she'd be through in a minute. It gave me time to see she'd done some yardwork since I was last there. It looked pretty good in bright sunlight that reflected off some of the floating flora roiled by the mower

She cut the engine after one last pass. "I don't do this as often as Fred used to," she said. "Every once in a while the neighbors complain. They take the landscaping seriously. Afraid I'm bringing down property values, I guess." I glanced at the adjacent yards. They were very well tended indeed.

"The Hackers spent a ton of money on landscaping last year."

"Hackers?" I interrupted.

"That's their name," she said gesturing to her left. They put in some nice flower beds, plantings, landscape timbers and all. They even put a coy pond in the back. Fixed it up real nice." She paused. "They had some heavy equipment in. Made a racket. Wake us up early and go on all day. Pissed Fred off." She brushed some dust from her jeans.

"Since then they make no secret of their displeasure at my letting the yard go from time to time. Even left a couple of nasty notes."

"It's why I live in a condo. Why don't you get a neighborhood kid to do it for you?" I asked. "You're getting a little long in the tooth for this kind of thing."

"Thanks for the compliment," she said showing a trace of irritation that showed through her florid cheeks. "Come on inside."

I waited in the living room while she washed some of the dust off and changed clothes. I admired some photographs on one wall I had not noticed during my previous visit. Some of them were pretty good shots taken around the city. They were all black and white with nice use of shadows and subtle shading. I always found black and white photos more interesting and artistic than color. I recognized many of the buildings and park scenes. When Mary returned I asked, "Did you shoot these? They're pretty good."

She stood silently for a moment looking nostalgic and sad at the same time. "No. Fred," she said wiping her hands on her thighs. "When he retired, he bought a camera...a nice one. He thought he'd take it up as a hobby. Got pretty good at it. He'd take off all day. Come back, put pictures on the computer. Email them someplace and have prints made of the best ones the same day." She paused reflectively. "He thought he'd set up a darkroom, but it never went that far."

"I thought you said he didn't have any hobbies."

"This didn't really count. He kind of cooled on it after a while. Said it was getting too expensive." She paused. "I don't know what he did with the camera. I guess he sold it."

"Yeah, it can become an expensive pastime," I said remembering an old second hand Leica I had once played with, producing nothing more than snapshots of friends and their pets.

She brought coffee. We sat and I told her about my conversation with Ansini. I repeated my feelings that this was going nowhere and that I couldn't see my way forward. I told her what Ansini had told me, that the best she could hope for would be someone coming forward with something. I told her I thought that was unlikely. It pained me to say it and it clearly pained her to hear it. Her lips trembled and eyes glistened as she fought back tears

She asked me to "think on it" and I promised I would as she gave me a hug and thanked me for trying. Leaving her at the front door I left, grateful to be out of it. I headed for some Boodles to celebrate. I could feel her watching me as walked to my car. Why was I feeling guilty?

The drive back to the condo featured a study in contrasts. The sun that had been so stunningly bright in Mary's yard was being erased by an enormous black cloud escorted by dramatic flashes of lightning and the roaring applause of thunder. Within a matter of seconds a wave of fat rain drops splashed on my windshield. Normally, I welcomed what I called "a good car washing rain." But this was more than that. Wipers could not keep up with it. Headlights could not penetrate the wall of water driven by a lusty wind that shook the old Corolla. I had to pull over. I don't think I'd ever had to do that before in the city although I had many times on the highway. At least here I didn't have to worry about eighteen wheelers speeding dangerously by, challenging the storms and the dismal visibility.

Sitting out a storm is not what I might have thought would be a good time to think of things beyond the storm itself. I had left Mary's happily. I had answered her call, come up with nothing, and reported what I had...or had not...learned. She took it well enough. But the tinge of guilt had stuck with me. As I sat listening to the drumbeat of rain, the rolling thunder and the startling lightshow, I found myself, as Mary had implored, involuntarily "thinking on it."

Two things were turning over in my mind like a slowly stirred batter. Pissed off and pictures. It occurred to me that these were new ingredients in the Fred Haller cake. He had gotten angry at a neighbor. Was that anger reciprocated? And, he took pictures. A hobby that was not a serious hobby, but that ostensibly might have taken him places he might otherwise not go. I was as intrigued by these thoughts as I was dismayed that I could feel myself being drawn back into the Fred Haller story like metal shavings to a magnet. I tried to make myself forget it but I couldn't.

By the time the storm had released holding me captive, I had decided to make up my mind what to do in consultation with my old friend Boodles. I turned the key to continue my way home. Nothing happened. The car was dead. My date with Boodles was delayed while I dialed Triple-A. Thank god I had my cell phone with me. Maybe it was worth a hundred bucks a month after all.

It was with admitted surprise that Mary took my call the next morning and with something more than enthusiasm when I told her I had a couple of ideas concerning Fred I wanted to talk over with her. I didn't tell her exactly what I had in mind, and told her not to get her hopes up, but said that we should probably talk. She was in a sooner-the-better mode.

A few minutes later I was in my newly battered car and on my way, wondering if this were the right thing. I was running the risk of raising expectations without any solid foundation. Disappointment could be damaging to Mary. Did I want to be a part of that? On the other hand, if I could give her some peace...a concluding chapter to the story...that would be worthwhile and satisfying, to me, and I thought, to her. Were my earlier doubts being buoyed by hope? I remembered a notable line from a Travis McGee story when his buddy Meyer told him.... "In all emotional conflicts, the thing you find the most difficult to do, is the thing that you should do." I thought to myself, be careful Trav. Be careful.

She was standing waiting at the wide open front door when I pulled up. She greeted me with a big smile and a generous hug. She guided me inside to the now familiar living room. "The coffee's on. I'll bring some in. I can't wait to hear what you have to tell me." A quick do-si-do and a minute later we were facing each other.

"Well?" she asked.

"Mary. I want to be sure you understand that what I'm about to say will not make much sense, and certainly will not provide the kind of answers you're looking for. Chances are remote they will. But," I paused, "they may give us another avenue besides Detective Ansini. And...they may not."

I looked at her with as sincere and serious an expression as I could muster. "It's important that you understand that, and that you not get those proverbial hopes up that anything could lead to anything. It's only an option that might...I repeat...might have some value." Her eyes got bigger. Somehow all I could think of at the moment was Churchill's description of Russia...*a riddle, wrapped in a mystery, inside an enigma.* That's what this challenge was all about.

"Okay Trav, I get it." She said it impatiently. "What's your idea?"

"Two things. I want to have a look at all of your husband's photos. And, I want to talk to the Hackers."

She looked befuddled. "Pictures? Hackers? I don't get it."

"I don't expect you to at this stage. Let me play it close to the vest for a bit then I'll explain. If there's anything to explain. Again, we're talking longshot here. Big time longshot."

I could see the disappointment. She was primed for meat and I gave her tofu. Hope exited stage left. Confusion took center stage. She wrung her hands as if trying to chase frostbite. Her head drooped until her chin almost touched her chest. A big deep breath then, "Okay Trav. Your call. Let me just tell you the photos will be no problem. The Hackers may be something else again. There's some bad blood there. Neighbor squabble stuff. I don't know how you get to them but I think you'll have to be on your own there. I'm not exactly the one to be making introductions."

"I can manage that. Is it the landscaping friction?"

She told me it was, and that feelings ran a little deeper than she might have indicated the other day. Fred was pissed. Really pissed. And, it led to some sharp words. No threats but a pretty good barrage of four letter words, and some longer than that, lobbed back and forth across the back fence. Robert Frost...I thought...good fences *were supposed* to make good neighbors.

I asked if she could put the photos from their computer onto a disc. No problem except she had no discs. I drove to the nearest Office Depot and acquired a package including more CDs than Mary and I could ever expect to use in a lifetime. We had a little trouble matching our technological expertise to the point where we could actually make the transfer, but we finally figured it out. She was better at that sort of thing than I was.

Afterwards, she made more coffee and sandwiches and we sat down in her kitchen. It reminded me of days gone by. A plastic tablecloth, an earlier decade's version of refrigerator, stove, microwave and sink. Very dated. The wrecking crew from HGTV would love to get their hands on this place. But, the coffee was good, and served today in mugs, not tea party crockery. The sandwiches were edible but reminded me of what they served at the Salvation Army when they were saving souls one sandwich at a time.

"Want to tell me what you're going to do with those pictures? she asked.

"Nope."

That took us into small talk mode. We talked about the so called old days at the television station. We reminisced about old colleagues and the kind of personalities that drifted into and out of the medium. We talked about what we saw today and discovered that neither of us could stomach local news broadcasts. We had the same complaints; too much crime, too little substance, too much meaningless banter, too little diversity. She was behind the scenes back in the day, but she was sharp and saw a lot of what was going on then with the same kind of perception with which she observed today's media world.

"You were one of the good ones," she said.

"I only did what I was told," I said. "I wanted to get out a number of times. But you know what they say about golden handcuffs. Too much money to walk away. Too much ego, yada, yada, yada."

"Remember Carson what's his name? He would not go on the street to do an interview without his studio makeup. Whenever I saw him I wanted to sing 'I Feel Pretty...the Little Richard version...not Rita Moreno."

"And, pretty girls," she said coyly.

"There was that," I said. "There was that."

"What was it between you and that cute reporter? I thought you would marry her."

That one came out of a very blue left field. I thought about it for a moment. "I almost did." She leaned back in apparent surprise.

"Jennifer?" She nodded.

"You didn't know it, but I was engaged to Jennifer."

"Jennifer Lewis? Wasn't that her name?"

"That Jennifer. I'm surprised you picked up on the relationship. But, maybe not. You seemed to know everything about that newsroom."

She shook her head. "Poor thing."

To me it was more than that. Jennifer and I had had a long relationship, but we had kept it very much off the radar. Management frowned on office romance. When it happened openly, one or the other...or both...found themselves "at liberty." That usually meant moving on to other, and invariably separate markets. And it that usually meant the end of the relationship.

That didn't happen to me and Jennifer. She moved on more tragically when a helicopter she was in on assignment went down. Nothing left at the end but a pile of ashes. In a few fateful seconds, a bright light went out, and I lost my way. I didn't allow Mary in on all of that. Too much booze, a little dope, and a long drop into an emotional abyss.

It took a very special lady to drag me out. We met on assignment. She worked for a nonprofit. It was non-profit all right because the boss was shuttling funds into a private account. Holly was instrumental in getting me the information I needed to bring in the story. I used to call her Holly Golightly thanks to Truman Capote. She did not go lightly from the non-profit, however, but rather heavily when they fired her for her loyalty to the truth rather than to the scoundrel. We married two months later and had a few years before the Big-C targeted her liver and clawed the life out of her.

Bringing back the thoughts of these months and years of my lifetime was a downer for me. And it took only seconds. I'm still not over any of it. But this was my story. All for me. Not Mary.

I thanked Mary for the lunch and the CD and told her to sit tight. I was going to do what I was going to do and I didn't know how long it was going to take. And I said, "If you see me in the neighborhood, don't be surprised. And don't say hello. I'm a stranger. Got it?"

There was sort of a gulp, a shrug, and a good-bye. I left fighting back tears for Jennifer, Holly and Mary. And for me.

I do have a life and friends and other things that I do. One of my best friends is Jeff Carr. He's a contemporary. Also a widower. He'd spent a lifelong career as a bureaucrat in the county election office shuffling papers. That was perfect for his reticent personality. He looked like he'd lived a life that didn't involve any heavy lifting; physical lifting that is. Soft hands and no wrinkles. His most striking feature was his eyebrows. They were snow white, like heavy frost that would have worked well in Dr. Zhivago.

He was a gentle soul, and was one of life's observers, one who didn't always appear to be paying attention and who seemed content to watch from the sidelines. But, when he joined the game, whatever it might be, he proved that he was able to carry his own weight and that he'd been listening and watching all the while. He proved that more than once as a bureaucrat and fought no holds barred when the Secretary of State was pushing for stronger voter ID laws that would have tossed a lot of people off the voter registration rolls.

He was an easy friend. No drama.

We see each other a couple of times a week, go to a movie, play backgammon, watch TV or have a pint or two at a favorite pub, Nellie's Place. It was middle class. Working class. Enough so to keep the yuppies away and the drinks reasonable. It did a brisk middle of the day and middle of the afternoon business with inexpensive beer and good sandwiches catering to retirees and shift workers.

It also featured a regular denizen who was more than a regular. His name was Andy. That's about all any of us knew about him. He was a fixture, like the big ceiling fan that whirred silently overhead as if watching customers. That job apparently belonged to Andy Whatshisname. No one but Nellie would know for sure. It seemed he was just in place to keep his eye on customers, and perhaps to make sure no one bothered her. At first glance one could be forgiven if doubting he could help in a pinch. He had to be seventy. His pinched face was heavily wrinkled but looked as if it had been chiseled out of stone. His hair was thin, his complexion the kind of gray that is sometimes caused by medication. His clothes always looked clean but faded from years of wear and washing. Andy never drank at Nellie's. I never saw him eat.

When regulars entered Nellie's they always nodded to Andy and he always nodded back. Newcomers got the onceover. The nods would come later if they ever came back. But perhaps his most striking feature was the baseball bat that rested on the chair next to him as he sat watching, and perhaps waiting.

It was at Nellies that Jeff and I caught up that afternoon. I told him what was going on and he rolled his eyes, suggesting that I was very much on a fool's errand.

"You're no more suited for this than I am for joining the Space Force," he said. One of his sons was a sheriff's deputy in Colorado so I suspect Jeff thought that he had some insight that he felt escaped me. "If I told him what you were up to," he said, "I know he'd tell me to tell you to find something else to do. Leave the cops' work to the cops."

He did not know Mary. He thought I was smitten with her. I explained that I was not, but did feel sorry for her. I tried to convince him that I'd just play the two hands I had, and gracefully bow out when they produced nothing as I fully expected to be the case.

Then we drifted into his world. He told me his son was thinking about leaving law enforcement. Too much pressure on the good guys who the public weren't seeing as very good these days. Too many young black men shot by cops under questionable circumstances. Too few cases of officers facing consequences.

Black Lives Matter activists were putting the squeeze on. Hands Up Don't Shoot protestors were all over the place. Cops were quitting and young men and women were turning their backs on the recruiting posters. Local law enforcement ranks were thinning, making it harder to police, much less maintain a viable and visible presence in those neighborhoods where crime was heaviest.

I questioned whether poor black neighborhoods even wanted cops around. Mothers feared that it could result in their kid being killed. Cops were often seen as the enemy. The dilemma, of course, is that the people who live in the toughest neighborhoods are the ones most in need of the help good law enforcement could provide.

"But as I see it," I said, "this is a lot more complicated than putting more cops on the street in high crime or poor neighborhoods. The pattern's the same all over the country. Too many kids are born into single parent poverty with two strikes against them before they leave the womb. They grow up fearing cops, admiring the guys on the corner with the bulging wallets and the crack and the heroin. Their parent or parents don't care. Their schools are shitty. They borrow electricity from the folks next door with stolen extension cords. There are no doctors and no supermarkets closer than a bus ride away. And even if there were, there's no money to pay the fare or buy much of anything. That's because there are no real jobs. Minimum wage. No job training. Try raising a family on nine or ten bucks an hour. Ten dollars an hour. That's four hundred a week if...if you're lucky enough to have something more than a part time gig. Twenty-something a year. Good luck with that."

"Trav. Nice job of stereotyping. So that's the way you see all of them?"

"Jeff did you say 'them'? Talk about stereotyping."

Jeff rubbed his forehead as if deep in thought. "Increasing the minimum wage ain't gonna happen. Some states and cities have kicked it up a bit, but the increases take a couple of years to go into effect. Kicking it up to fifteen bucks an hour still doesn't put you on the stairway to paradise."

"Money, or lack of it," I said, "Isn't the whole story. There are other changes that are just as important. Pre-school education, nutrition programs, access to health care. Finding ways to motivate kids and families who are now only motivated by all the wrong things. If they're motivated at all and haven't given up. Add to this the fact guns are everywhere. Desperate teenagers have them. And as we read every day and see on TV, they are not afraid to use them. They mug someone or hold up a convenience store because they're hungry, or need clothes so they don't feel embarrassed in school, or mom's sick, or dad needs to be bailed out. Or just for kicks. Bingo, they're in jail.

"Most can't make bail. They wait for a year to go to trial and lose their jobs...if they had one. Many wind up in solitary. Do you know what solitary does to a young brain...a brain that's not yet fully formed? That's what gets them into trouble in the first place. The part of the young brain that puts up the stop sign when it comes to risky behavior is just not there yet. So they run through the stop light."

"Relax Trav. You don't have to convince me."

I gave the bar a good thump with the flat of my hand attracting the attention of some of the drinkers nearby. A black busboy was watching out of the corner of his eye as he wiped a table nearby.

"Whew...what unleashed that McGee?" Jeff looked at me strangely. "That's a bona fide rant. I watch the news. You're preaching to the choir. Tells me you should be spending your time writing letters to the editor not trying to play Sherlock Holmes."

"I've written a few," I said, but I was not through. "It's all a vicious circle that we've got to break at the beginning. Not the middle or the end.

It'll take a generation to change. Politicians won't do it. It'll have to be organic from the ground up." I took a big swallow of beer. "End of lecture."

"Good," came a voice from behind us. "I've been listening to your bullshit, nigger lover." The busboy retreated into the kitchen.

"You've got it all wrong," said the voice. Jeff sat straight up in his chair.

"These people don't want to work. They just care about handouts, and fucking, and killing honkies. I say throw them in jail and toss the keys. Better yet, they ought to all be sent back to Africa...you know, the 'shithole countries.' Perfect for them." He paused to crack his knuckles. Snap, click, snap, one seemed more threatening than the other.

I could see Andy out of the corner of my eye. The bat was now on his lap. A bony hand flexed around the handle. His expression said "We don't want any trouble here, but if it comes, I'm ready."

The guy who owned the snapping, crackling fingers, was big and burly and bald. His face was heavily jowled. A ball of putty turned out to be a nose featuring a road map of tiny blood vessels, directions to bushy, gray eyebrows. Surprisingly, his eyes were hiding behind wire glasses that would have been more at home perched on the nose of an accountant. Dirty jeans were hoisted over a beer belly by wide suspenders flirting with a maximum load. He looked like he was in his sixties and like he didn't have a lot of nickels to rub together. I knew that under his sweat shirt there was undoubtedly a tattoo that read "Mother" or "Semper Fi." I hoped it was "Mother."

And, he was not finished. "My parents came from the old country with nothing. They worked hard. No handouts, and brought us up good. We didn't need no welfare. I don't want my tax money going to freeloaders."

He looked like he wanted to punch me in the nose and he probably did. "These people get too much from the government. I was in Nam. I didn't fight for handouts to niggers."

So it would be Semper Fi I thought. "Easy on the "N" word buddy. That doesn't work anymore. And, I'll guess that some black buddies had your back more than once." If looks could kill.

"Coon work better for you mother fucker?"

"Nope. White trash work for you?"

Jeff shifted uneasily in his chair.

A momentary standoff. The room went silent. Andy was now standing, rigid like a statue. Some good old boys who were likely drinking buddies of the big guy edged closer to us. More Semper Fi tattoos under wraps. They didn't look like they were interested in the finer points of debate. I thought there was a good chance this could get even uglier quickly.

And while I was not interested in any bloodshed, I could not resist.

"Think about it if you've ever cashed an unemployment check, known a family on food stamps, cashed a Social Security check or slipped your Medicare card to the doc." He was really into my space now. "Some people call that welfare."

"I earned them," he said, "by working all my life." His friends nodded some of them mumbling, "That's right."

I went on. "And paying taxes. Poor people pay taxes. That's how Uncle Sam pays for programs that help them. Their taxes, yours and mine. And, when it works just right, poor people do better and pay more taxes." I was trying to sound cool and calm. I'm not sure I looked it.

I continued. "Government programs probably helped your parents. If so, I bet they didn't call it welfare." I turned to Jeff as the other guy was apparently momentarily out of words. He waved his hand at me. I wasn't sure if it was a dismissive gesture or whether he was winding to throw a punch. Whatever, the body language did not suggest a hug. I signaled Jeff it was time to go and tossed a ten spot on the table.

The big man was apparently through and surprisingly stood aside though I did not miss the fact that he still clenched and unclenched his fists as if he were squeezing a lemon. I said to Jeff as we started for the door, "And that guy's mindset," I said pointing with a thumb over my shoulder, "is exactly why the things we've been talking about will not change during our lifetimes."

I nodded toward the big guy and his pals as we walked past. "There are just too many of him in this world, and not enough of us. Let's go." We got past him and his friends, knowing they, and we, were all too old to change. Andy sat down and relaxed his hold on the Louisville Slugger as he watched us leave.

Jeff was shaking his head as we breathed deeply in relief in the afternoon fresh air. "I thought he might take a punch at you," he said. "Did you see how red he got in the face?" He laughed nervously. "More to the point, I thought he might take a swipe at me."

"Yeah, I did too. Glad he didn't. He'd have killed me then wiped up the mess with you. Not a pretty picture." I stopped suddenly. I had just given myself an idea.

"Hey, if you've got an hour or so, why don't you come to my place. I've got a bunch of photographs I have to look at. Maybe you can help me find what I'm looking for. Whatever that is."

He smiled. "Sure. I've got nothing but time." As we started toward my car he said, laughing, "If you're going to wrangle me into this caper of yours, this Mary had better be cute?"

"You're way too old for that kind of talk," I said. "Maybe there'll be a picture of her for you to decide for yourself."

I poured us both a drink before sitting down at the computer. He stuck with beer. I poured a small Boodles thinking it was five-o-clock someplace. Jeff pulled up a chair and watched me insert the CD into the computer, wave the mouse across the mouse pad, click a few keys, and open up Fred's file.

"Whoa." Jeff said what I was feeling. "That looks like a lot of pictures."

"They're all in color. I'm a little surprised. The ones he framed at home are in black and white."

One by one we went through them. He liked scenic shots. Landscapes and buildings. Parks, featuring geese and pigeons. Occasional homeless people asleep on cardboard pallets and benches, or begging on street corners. He ventured out to the airport more than once and went overboard snapping planes taking off and landing.

We recognized many of the downtown landmarks. There didn't seem to be anything remarkable about any of them as we went through the photos one by one. I recognized a couple that he liked well enough to have had printed and framed. We studied the pictures for more and an hour, a process that was tedious and tired our eyes.

"Another beer?" Jeff seemed close to nodding off.

"Thanks. If I do, I'll really fall asleep. But sure."

"We only have a few more. Let's take a short

break before we finish up. Still have time?"

"Sure." Good old Jeff.

I got the drinks and we turned away from the computer screen. We talked about what we had gone through so far and agreed that while there was nothing remarkable about the photos in general, there was also nothing that might even remotely suggest any connection with Fred's disappearance. He didn't seem interested in people, except for the few homeless folks, or unless they were in the foreground or background of one of his metropolitan architectural still lifes.

"He must have shot every building downtown," said Jeff.

"Well, he was a glazier. Maybe he was admiring his handiwork."

"Or maybe studying to become a street person."

"Wise ass!"

We went back to the computer. More of the same. There were a couple of shots of a garden featuring a Bobcat with lots of attachments, piles of landscape timbers and some plantings. There was one small cement statue. Rodin's Thinker. I wondered what the heck it was doing there.

A few workmen were also in evidence. I suspected he had taken these photos while the neighbors were ensuring a higher property tax with all the backyard landscaping improvements. I wondered why he bothered. Maybe he thought he could use it to bolster his complaints.

No pictures of Mary. That struck me as a little odd. But maybe she was one of those women who didn't like to have their picture taken. Maybe he was not ready for the portrait phase of his budding hobby. Maybe a lot of things. No pictures of him either. Not surprising. He was the guy behind the camera. And, Fred never liked being "out there." With him it was always about Mary. He was quite content to stand aside. So...why no pictures of Mary?

After almost two hours of it we had gone through all of the photos. Jeff and I agreed that Fred Haller didn't show a lot of promise with the camera, and had probably done the right thing by giving up on his photographic ambitions.

"Well, after all of that, what do you think?" I asked Jeff as he took the final swallow of his beer.

"You sure know how to entertain a fellow," he said smiling. "Too bad. It would have been nice to see him with a ticket for one of those airplanes. Or curled up on a cardboard pallet." He shrugged his shoulders. "I think you're ready for phase two."

"Thanks anyway for the company. Sorry it wasn't more interesting."

"It's okay Trav. The beer was cold. And free. May I go now?"

"Your sentence is over."

I led him to the door and thanked him again.

Then I did something that surprised me. I went back to the computer and started through the pictures again. Same result. I don't know if I had a hunch that I had missed something or whether I was just trying to avoid another evening with my friends at CNN and enduring even more frustration watching the news of the day.

When I had finished I was right where I started. Nothing to see in the photographs beyond evidence of an older man trying to find a hobby and not being very good at it.

For some reason, I fell asleep that night wondering about two things that seemed a little out of the ordinary. Why so many pictures of the neighbor's yard? And, whatever happened to the camera? I remembered waiting for Mary to bring coffee during one of my visits. A large bookshelf was filled with the usual thrillers, old best sellers, ancient Reader's Digests and how-to books and magazines. One full shelf was devoted to books on photography. Most of them were quite expensive hardbacks unlike the mostly paperback others. My last waking thought was so what.

My first thought on waking up was I wished I were a fisherman so I could go fishing. My second thought was I wished I were a golfer so I could go golfing. Then I wished I were a monk so I could go into seclusion.

Then I went Googling and Facebooking. Why

not? I Googled "Fred Haller." And, I learned more than I needed to know about a pediatrician in Des Moines...a lawyer in Portland and a local mayor in Texas. They were the standouts among dozens of Fred Hallers living or dead. I should have known that a lifelong glazier was not likely to have much of an online profile.

Fred Haller had an even lesser presence on Facebook. I don't know what I thought I might find, beyond countless photos of cats or what a bunch of pathologically needy people had for breakfast or dinner, just to let the world know they existed. What was I thinking aside from just putting off the inevitable?

The first of the two ideas I had had about pursuing the ghost that Fred Haller had become was an apparent bust. Now, it was on to phase two. I needed to talk to the Haller neighbors, convinced that after that I would have to talk to Mary armed with the proper excuses to extricate myself from this self-imposed assignment. Then, perhaps, I might seriously think about taking up fishing, golf or joining a monastic order...as long it was one that made booze and could guarantee eternal life.

I had just put the morning coffee on when the phone rang. It was Mary. I was surprised. I don't know why.

"Find anything?" she asked before even saying hello. I recognized the voice.

"Well, hello to you too. Find anything what?"

"I thought you wanted to look for some ideas in his pictures. Have you looked at them yet?"

I told her I had gone through them twice and had found nothing that I found useful. "What were you looking for?" she asked. "Anything in particular?"

"I don't know what I was looking for. Maybe just hopeful that something would just pop up and give me something to go on."

She confirmed that the shots of the backyard landscaping project were indeed photos of the neighbor's yard.

"Why did he take so many shots of all of that?" I asked.

She paused before answering. "I really don't know. He never told me. I never asked. I do remember that he was really put off by the noise and the dust. He tried to get the Hackers to get the men to start later in the day. They more or less ignored him. It ticked him off." She went silent for a few seconds. "Maybe he was going to make an issue of it somehow, but I don't know what good the pictures would do."

"You've obviously seen his photos. Right Mary?"

"Sure. Most of them I guess."

"But you did know there were those shots of the...what's the name...Hackers...back yard."

"Yeah. But they didn't mean anything to me."

With a little laugh I told her that I was a bit surprised that there were no pictures of her. She said that I shouldn't be surprised, that she hated having her picture taken. She told me she hadn't had a picture of her taken of in years. Forty years ago she would have posed all day if asked. Now, as "an older woman" she didn't ever want to stand in front of a camera again. I commiserated. It's not one of my favorite things either. I told her that I would not be having pictures taken of me until they came up with an industrial strength Photoshop program so we could all look like teenagers again.

"I guess I'll stop by in the next day or two and have a chat with the Hackers. Do you want to introduce me?" I asked, pretty sure of her answer.

"No thanks. They can go jump in their new coy pond as far as I'm concerned. It would probably be a good idea to not even let them know that you know us. Fred did, I think, burn some bridges there."

"I'll figure it out," I said. In my own mind I knew that would not be a problem. I had my story all worked out.

My mind returned once again to the pictures. I don't know why I was intrigued by them. They were amateur photos taken by a guy who was missing. Practically speaking there was no reason to have any reasonable expectation there was anything in the photos that would help me understand what had happened to Fred Haller.

As much as I wanted to toss the whole matter back to Mary Haller and forget about all of it, I found myself, in a curious way, being drawn into it against my will. There was something fascinating about the disappearance. And, my involvement, even at this amateurish level, had a voyeuristic quality that I found somehow, on some level, appealing. Maybe it was just boredom and needing something to do.

Here I was looking into the lives of two people who were little more than acquaintances. I knew her as a former colleague who had supported me in a time of some stress. I hardly knew Fred at all. I wasn't even sure I'd recognize him if he walked into my home at that moment. And, of course, there were no pictures of him among his photographs to remind me. No surprise there. He was, after all the man behind the camera.

For some reason it made me think of Hitler's henchman Martin Bormann. Of him it was said that he prohibited anyone from taking his picture. Ostensibly, as chief of staff to Hitler, he wanted to remain anonymous because of his awareness of, and complicity in, the enormity of the Nazi leader's crimes. Certainly thoughts like these were unfair to Mary and Fred Haller. I felt guilty for its even having crossed my mind.

The sun was shining brightly as I pulled up outside the Hacker home. I hoped Mary had remembered to ignore me if she saw me around. No sign of her or of anyone except a lady walking what I assumed was a golden retriever half a block away. Both blondes.

I climbed four steps to the front door and rang the bell. No answer. I knocked. That produced a response not from inside the house, but from behind me.

"Hello. Is there something I can do for you."

I turned and the two blondes were at the bottom of the stairs. The dog looked very doglike. She looked like she could do a pretty good real estate deal. Trim. Nice clothes, nice smile, nice white teeth, nice diamond ring. Nice frosted hair.

I stepped down the steps toward her. "Oh, I'm sorry," I said. "This your place?"

She nodded and tightened her grip on the leash. I couldn't determine if it was a preamble to an order to attack or whether she was protecting me from a potentially over enthusiastic new buddy. I smiled in a way I hoped was reassuring and would allay any possible fears that I was an aging second story man, or even worse, a door to door salesman.

"What do you want?" She asked with a nice blend of friendliness and wariness with a little impatience thrown in for good measure. The dog was all friendly with a wagging tail with enough motion that he seemed capable of lifting ...I think it was a him...at least his backside off the ground.

"That looks like a pretty good boy you've got there," I said.

"It's Daisy," she responded, "and it's a she." She paused obviously waiting for an answer to her earlier question.

"Hi. My name is Tom McGee. Folks call me Trav. I know your neighbors the Hallers." I thought I saw her eyes roll ever so slightly when I mentioned the name. I hadn't planned on associating myself with Mary but thought if I mentioned the neighborhood connection she'd realize I was not someone bent on mischief. That, and my age, should have lessened any threat she might be feeling.

"I apologize for sort of stumbling by, but Mary told me you had some landscaping done a few months back. I was hoping I could take a look and maybe get some ideas. I've got the itch." I tried to give her the smile Bogey used in African Queen. She gave me an is this guy for real look. "I could come back another time," I added.

"This is not a great time," she answered. "I have to run some errands. You can walk around back and take a look if you like. But, if you have any questions you'll have to talk to Troy, my husband. It's his baby."

"Thanks, I'll do that. I can use some fine points. Horticulture is not my thing, but I do want to dress up my place. If you'll give me your number, I'll call ahead in a day or two and come by at your convenience."

She gave it to me more readily than I might have expected. I guess I had pulled it off. I took out my cell and punched in the number as she gave it to me.

"It's Troy and....?"

"Troy and Jennifer Hacker." I felt a twinge. I never heard the name Jennifer without that feeling as if someone had set off a tiny explosion in my heart. She added, "People call me Jenny."

She smiled. "I've got to run." She made a funny clicking sound that the dog responded to and they both bounced up the stairs, their backsides in unison.

She turned as she was shutting the door. "The best time to call, Mr. McGee, is at night. We're usually home." With that, she shut the door leaving me free to wander around. I suspect she was watching but I took care not to appear as if I were looking for her at the window.

I walked down the driveway and turned through a small gate near the garage. The garage door was open and I could see a nifty red Mercedes waiting to be saddled up and launched to the local grocery store. I don't know the Mercedes line very well, but guessed it was one of those models identified by letters and numbers and something close to a six figure price tag. She's running errands in that, I thought, reinforcing my earlier feeling that she was selling something in the high end real estate market.

It struck me as a little odd. The car did not match the house. It was the kind of vehicle you'd expect to find at the front door of a home the size of a library nestled behind high gates and fifteen foot tall shrubbery.

The Hacker place was on the modest size, maybe two thousand square feet stretched over two floors. A brick façade and siding. Plantation shutters did not match the style of the place. But it did have a big backyard and that's where I found myself.

While it was good sized, it was too small for all the trimmings. It made the Hanging Gardens of Babylon look fallow. Too many plantings for the space, few of which I could identify. Some berms has been created giving portions of the yard a contour that did not seem to fit. Some landscape timbers bordered the yard, with smaller versions around some of the plantings. There was an ample amount of knee and waist high cement and plaster statuary to make it difficult to walk in a straight line. I recognized some of the figures, copies of some unknown masters, and some known, like the Rodin. I spotted a cupid aiming an arrow toward the house. It gave me heartburn. I was tempted to turn it toward the Haller place as a gesture of neighborly love.

I was going to have to bone up on landscaping chatter before Troy and I did our thing. I was pretty much limited to terms like zoysia, fescue and crab grass. Mostly crab grass.

I spent the next ten minutes wandering around looking interested. I came upon the coy pond just as I heard about 150 horses blast off in the garage and propel a red flash down the driveway, roaring off to god knows where. The sound was gone quickly and I was left with the silence of growing things, and of a dog barking inside the house. Daisy was doing her job. Time to go. My reconnoitering mission now completed. I was attentive to the little pond as I left. A couple of big gold fish and I exchanged glances as I stepped by cautiously and mindfully.

I called the Hackers the next night. Troy was friendly, especially after I was so enthusiastic about how much I admired his landscaping. He wondered though why I could not ask my questions about what I wanted to know over the phone. I explained that I didn't know the names of some of the things I was interested in talking about, suggesting it would be hard to describe them long distance. His own pride over what he had wrought on "the Back 40" as he called it, was sufficient to prompt an invitation for Saturday morning. I thought to myself that all the crap he had in the "Back 40" was more than enough for a plot twice the size.

I showed up at ten with a bag of donuts which

prompted what felt like a reluctant invitation for coffee before we went to the "Back 40." It gave us time to chat.

Troy was a nice looking guy. Fit and trim. Maybe thirty or so. His wife may have been a year or two older. Though cute in a perky sort of way, the sweep of her Saturday mid-morning makeup made her look as if she were trying to hide something, like early onset crows feet and nascent jowls.

I was right. She was in real estate and was happy to tell me she had rewarded herself for a couple of really big sales, and one especially big one, with that nice red car in the garage. Troy was "in insurance." Somehow I had the feeling that he was not up to her speed in the sales department and that it would be a long, long time before the "nice red car" had a running mate. I was speculating, but I had to give them credit supposing they had solved a problem for which there must have been some testy negotiations. I guessed that when they split the baby...her big commission check...she got custody of the car, he got the "Back 40."

I brought up the Hallers. Not reluctantly, because the real purpose of my visit was to get their take on the neighbors, especially Fred. But I was wary because of the bad blood Mary had told me about.

I told them I had taken a good look at their yard previously, and was grateful that Mary Haller had told me about the work they had done. Jenny and Troy exchanged quick glances when I mentioned Mary's name. There was something in the brief exchange that made me think Jenny didn't want Troy to say anything. And, there was also something that made me think that it was beyond his not saying anything. More like you'd better not...or else. I was surprised when he did.

She sat with her arms folded, tapping her foot.

Troy looked at her and cleared his throat. He seemed nervous. "They were quite a couple. I say were, because he's no longer around, but I suppose you know that."

I nodded my yes.

"I'd have to say that on those rare occasions when I saw them together, they looked like a young couple. Hand in hand. Arm in arm and all that."

I don't know why that was a bit of a surprise. Good for them I thought. Jenny wasn't reacting. She looked like she wanted a cigarette or something stronger. She was casting a chill over the room.

Troy went on. "He was a real pain in the ass when I was doing the landscaping." With that, Jenny harrumphed and left the room.

"She doesn't like me using that kind of language."

I would bet that she could do him a lot better on that count if tested or provoked.

He went on. "He complained all the

time...threatened to sue. Too much dust and dirt. Too much noise from the heavier equipment. Some of the workmen joked and cursed and drank beer when they were shutting down the job for the day. He didn't like that. But they were good guys and did a good job. I actually thought Haller was nuts. A couple of the landscape guys were Hispanic. And he asked if they all had papers."

So that's why he was taking pictures I thought to myself. He planned to report them. I wonder if he did.

"Strange. Had there been any issues before that?" I asked. I wanted to keep him talking without seeming more interested than I should have been.

"No. No problem. We did get on them from time to time about their yard. They let it go. It looked kind of shabby a lot of the time. Grass going to seed and all that. We told them they were bringing property values down. Other than that, not much contact at all. I mean, they were both older. Not much in common. You know..." A sudden pained expression. His voice trailed off in embarrassment.

"Well, I don't know them all that well. I worked with Mary years ago. I ran into her downtown and she invited me over for coffee. We got to talking and she mentioned your landscape project. I was glad it came up. She got really upset when talking about Fred. I was glad when the subject changed."

"That was a weird one. Now you see him, now you don't. Did they ever find out what happened to him?"

"Nope. It's driving her crazy."

"She was okay. Never complained about any of it. Just him."

I sat there silently. Sometimes silence can be a real conversation starter. People, especially when nervous, get uncomfortable with the silence and feel they have to say something to break it. He did.

"Let's go out to the "Back 40," he said.

The number of plantings had not gotten any smaller since my earlier visit, nor had the size of the space gotten larger. So we sidestepped our way around statues, bushes, saplings and other growing things. He told me how he planned it all out himself without benefit of a landscape architect. I was not surprised and told him what a good job he'd done. He beamed and started in on how much he's saved by doing it that way bringing down the overall cost considerably. Without batting an eyelash he said, "I saved a bunch by using the spics too." I thought that maybe Fred was on to something about Troy being a jerk.

There was more talk about expenses including the confirmation that Jenny got the better end of the deal when it came to divvying up her commission money. But I couldn't believe what he'd put into it. It was an expensive project.

Troy liked to talk and was fluent in the language of landscaping. He pointed out the attributes of this and that and was very proud of the statuary he had collected. He had already proved that he was also fluid in the language of prejudice. I was almost expecting him to say he loved "wop" sculptors or "Jewed-down" the sellers. He didn't go that far.

"Look. There's Mary watching us from the window."

Troy pointed with his chin toward the Haller house. There indeed was Mary watching from a curtained window. I don't know if she was waving, or just letting the curtain close. I gave a little wave but there was no response. It gave me a chance to get back to my mission. I wanted to get out of Troy's hair and his crummy way too expensive "Back 40."

Troy opened a door for my departure...exposing what I considered an ever more obvious insensitivity. "Poor Mary. Jenny and I used to wonder if she killed Fred and buried him in the basement or stuffed him in the attic. Just disappearing like that. Weird."

"Don't you think they got along?" I was fishing.

"I think they did get along. Like I said before. Lots of hand in hand walks."

"Like you and Jenny I'll bet," I said smiling hoping the sarcasm wasn't all that obvious. He smiled. He either got it or thought he might hit me up for an insurance policy.

On cue Jenny came out to join us. I suppose it was to tell all by her presence that all was forgiven for Troy's having used the word "ass" in front of her and me.

Troy held out his hands as if receiving a debutante. "Trav and I were just talking about Fred. What do you think's the story there?"

"He bolted," she said coldly. "I think he got tired of whatever life he...they...had and moved on. He was nutty, but not an Alzheimer's case. He just left. That's what I think."

She looked toward the Haller home. "I was going to bring her over a bowl of soup or something when he left...disappeared. But, she was upset. I didn't want to bother her.

Yeah, she was upset I thought. She was childless, without a lot of friends and her husband was gone. She sure didn't want to be "bothered" by a bitch who couldn't go to the trouble of driving her million dollar car to the local supermarket for a bowl of fucking soup!

But, I was grateful. Jenny had opened the Pandora's box. I was interested how she discussed the lives of other people as effortlessly as she might explain the benefit of an open floor plan.

Troy looked and sounded like he was enjoying this little game. "The cops were in and out for a couple of days. They spoke with us once or twice. They wanted to know if we had seen or heard anything that might tell them something. That's when I began thinking body in the basement because it seemed like they were thinking that way. I was thinking Alfred Hitchcock. From what I understand, his wallet, credit cards and cash were found inside long after he left."

He turned to Jenny. "You don't bolt without those things Jenny."

She glared at him. "When it's time to go it's time to go. You can find a way." That was her story and she was sticking to it. I could see that she would not be fun to argue with. Perkiness could turn to steel...a polite smile could become icy in an instant.

I said, "The cops seem to have come down on the notion he had early onset Alzheimer's or dementia, wandered off, and maybe fell into the river."

They looked at each other.

"He bolted!"

"Dig up the basement. Look in the attic."

Troy and Jenny. Cute couple! I thanked them for the tour and, I hate to say it, I bolted. However, I left knowing nothing more than I arrived with other than the fact that this couple was not going on my Christmas card list, and that I would never leave my condo so I could have a place with a garden.

The landline was ringing as I opened the door to my place. It was Mary. "I saw you in the Hacker jungle," she said. "Quite a place isn't it? Way too busy."

"That's putting it mildly. Quite a couple too."

"She runs the show. I'll bet she hates that garden."

"But loves the car." I paused. No response. "I think you should know I told them that we know each other. I needed to reassure her that I had some standing in the neighborhood when she found me on her porch."

"That's okay by me."

In language as delicate as I could muster, I told her about the conversations and how Jenny was convinced Fred had just taken off, while Mark was convinced he was six feet under in the basement or mummified in the attic. Her response was colorful, purple being the first color that came to mind, language no doubt that she had picked up in the newsroom. I thought Jenny would not last five minutes in a room with Mary with that kind of talk.

She said, "That makes as much sense as my suggesting they killed Fred to stop his complaining and buried him in that awful garden."

I was struck that she could even say "killed Fred." I found even a tacit suggestion from Mary that Fred could be dead...murdered...a little odd and unsettling. I guess after all these months she was accepting the reality that he could no longer be alive.

"Troy is convinced that Fred was likely to make a thing out of the landscapers...the Hispanics. Call the authorities or something. Anything to that?"

"He did mention something once about them possibly being illegals. But he'd never follow up. Where do you go with something like that? He thought he could intimidate Troy. He just wanted a little peace and quiet...nine to five instead of seven to seven.

"I don't think we should make too much of the squabble. It was just that...a squabble. No big deal in the scheme of things. It can't have anything to do with Fred's going missing.

"Which brings me to the point Mary. I can't think of anything I can do. As a reporter I would say, I can't advance the story. Unless there's something we haven't discussed...something that might be relevant."

There was a long silent pause. I was dismayed and yet relieved, when I heard a definitive click breaking the connection. I thought to myself well, that's that. Not even a goodbye.

It was some weeks later, with Mary and Fred Haller very much in my rear view mirror, when I was at Nellie's waiting for Jeff. He'd been away and had called saying he wanted to "catch up." Another way of saying let's have a drink. I had just taken delivery of a pint of Foster's when I looked up to see Detective Paul Ansini come through the door. He stood there as if he were looking for someone when I caught his eye and waved. He clearly didn't recognize me at first. Then he ambled over.

"McGee right?"

"You got it. Good memory Detective Ansini. Have a seat. I'll buy you a beer."

"No thanks. I'm supposed to meet someone here." Just then his phone chirped La Marseillaise. He pulled it out of his pocket and studied it for a moment.

"False alarm. My meeting just texted. Called it off." He pulled out a chair and sat down. "No beer. I'm still on duty, but I will take a cup of coffee." I signaled the waiter.

We made a little small talk as we waited, agreeing that it was a nice day and that the Cardinals still had a crack at the pennant. Nellie herself brought the coffee and I joked that good help was hard to find. Ansini took sugar and cream and while he stirred slowly he said, "I heard from what's her name...Mary Haller today."

I was surprised to hear her name. She'd been off my radar for a month or more.

"I thought you were going to solve the case for us," he said sarcastically. "She's pretty insistent that we come up with something. I can't seem to convince her that this case has frost on it. Nothing for us to go on until somebody or something gives us someplace to go."

"I had a little trouble convincing her of that too. I guess I understand what she's going through." I took a swallow of my beer. "I did try to look into some things for her, but there was nothing there.

"He took a lot of pictures around town, and had occasional words with the neighbors, but that was about it. The pictures didn't amount to much. The folks next door were just noisy." Ansini looked bored. Who wouldn't be?

I needed to talk about something so I continued. "He thought some Hispanics working on the neighbor's yard might be undocumented. He apparently threatened to quote 'go to the authorities' to put a little pressure on the neighbors. Where would he go with a complaint like that?"

"The feds. Homeland Security. They run the Custom's Enforcement folks. We wouldn't be involved...at least we don't want to be involved. Christ, that's all we'd need is to have to deal with that crap. It's all very sensitive with a lot of loose threads as to what local cops should and should not do on illegals. A Pandora's box if we start helping ICE. We start making raids with ICE...trouble ahead."

"Why's that?" I asked. "I always thought law enforcement birds of a feather and all..."

"The immigrant community already distrusts

cops. A lot of them from other countries had real problems with them. That's what they ran away from. Illegals are a dime a dozen around here. They don't bother anybody. They work hard. Live and let live I say. And, the feds already have enough to worry about at the border. Laws are different all over the country. The courts are trying to un-scramble it everywhere."

"Okay, for the sake of discussion, let's say the workers got wind of Fred Haller's concerns. Or their bosses did. You can get into some trouble hir-ing undocumented workers. Right?"

"Sure. There are fines. Small first time around, but they can add up. And, there can be jail time." He looked at me questioningly. "Are you thinking what I think you're thinking."

"Hypothetical, as I said, just for discussion. Can I make a scenario like...the company honchos get nervous when someone starts saying things that could bring in the feds? They have a talk with Fred Haller. It doesn't go well, and suddenly they decide to make him part of somebody's garden. Like the deep part."

I was enjoying making all this up. I wasn't really serious when I began thinking out loud. At the same time I was aware that while it was an un-likely scenario it was one in which the pieces actu-ally could fit.

"Longshot McGee. Longshot. You're watching too much TV. Don't play Sherlock. My father used to say to me that 'when you don't know where you're going, any road will take you there.' You can get into trouble if you're not careful McGee. I gotta go. Fred Haller is probably face down in a creek or in the woods."

"Someone could have put him there," I said with a smile, trying not to look smart ass. He didn't return the smile. "McGee...you're too old for this sort of thing." The unkindest cut of all.

He left me with half a Foster's and an empty coffee cup. He walked out of Nellie's still shaking his head just as Jeff walked in. Although I realized the idea was probably over the top I thought I would give this newfound scenario a try on him. At least it would give us something to talk about...after catching up. Beats looking at pictures of the grandkids.

Jeff sauntered over to our table. I lifted a finger to Nellie. When she saw Jeff she nodded and headed for the bar to bring him a beer.

"Is the coast clear? No good old boys today?" We laughed as we shook hands.

I told him about my release from the Haller bondage, including the saga of the "Back 40." We had a good laugh. I was rewarded with a detailed recitation of his visit with the grandkids. When we ran out of all of that, I tried my latest round of deductive reasoning on him.

"What do you think?" I asked. I had warmed

to my fiction after the second telling and a second Foster's. Jeff had listened as quietly and politely as I had during his vacation update.

"Make a great movie," he said. "You don't really believe it do you? You made it up on the basis of what? That some Hispanic landscapers happened to work on a missing neighbor's back yard?" He looked at me as if to say snap out of it.

And, with this polite chiding my own enthusiasm dwindled. I realized I had concocted the scenario more for my own entertainment than as a viable story line. It was a twofer. Ansini and Jeff had double teamed me...separately but without hesitation. What was I thinking? I really had no interest in rekindling the Fred Haller story. I could not have been happier when Mary had hung up on me.

I must have looked deflated and dispirited. Jeff was not one to allow that for very long. Unexpectedly, he said, "So were these yard guys on their own or did they work for somebody?"

I was surprised he was going back to the fiction. "I don't know. I'm guessing they worked for somebody else."

"Hmm," he said, his white eyebrows lifting slightly. "If you're at all serious about this...this theory, then maybe it's worthwhile digging a little. A gang of gardeners might not even know there was a complaint or threat. Their boss, on the other hand..."

"...might be more concerned about the possibility of fines. Especially if it were a big company with a lot of undocumented types."

"Could be."

"Hah. I'll find out."

We left it at that. Good old Jeff. Another indication of the way old guys think when they have too much time on their hands, and too much beer in their bellies. We chatted some more about the more mundane things guys like us talk about like solving world problems, sports, and the latest Netflix series, eventually calling it a day.

That evening I made a call I really didn't want to make. After sunset I dialed the Hacker number. "This is Jenny Hacker," came at me loud and clear after one and a half rings. She's waiting for a call back on a real estate deal I thought. I told her who I was after a short pause that indicated two levels of disappointment; no sale and remembering me. She put some ice on the line with a very cool, "What do you want?" and an equally brusque, "He's not here," when I asked for Troy.

"Call after eight." She was curt. she said it like someone who wanted to give the impression of being helpful but didn't care if she was or not. I wanted to tell her that I was so impressed with their landscaping I wanted to use the same company. We didn't get that far. The call ended right on the word "eight" as she slapped the phone into its cradle with more than a little emphasis. I was surprised she had a landline. Behind the times, just like the rest of us. It was probably Troy's idea.

Troy was cordial when I finally reached him. He gave me the name of the firm who did the work and seemed slightly flattered when I said I wanted to contact the people who did all that good work for him. "The Green Grass of Home," he told me. I wondered what kind of person came up with that name?

I want to Google to continue my "research." I expected it to lead me to a website for a small local company.

Good old Google gave me more. The Green Grass of Home was a franchised subsidiary of a major landscape services company with franchise operators in several states and with overall annual revenues approaching several million dollars. And, it was not even near the top of the list of big money-making companies. Obviously, to generate that kind of money, it had to have a lot of franchisees who performed a wide variety of services for individual home owners, commercial concerns and many local, state and national government properties. Services included a lot more than mowing lawns and planting bushes. The company could do anything in a backyard from swimming pools, conservation counseling, outdoor kitchens, fencing, walls, decks, outdoor lighting, pest control and on and on. So, The Green Grass of Home was really a small part of something big called National American Landscape, Inc. I had never heard of it. But National American Landscape, Inc.'s main office was in our backyard, about five miles from where I was sitting at the moment I learned of its existence. I found myself wondering how many employees it had, how many Hispanic, and how many might have been undocumented?

My, my.

I couldn't resist driving by the next day. For such a big operation, the building was not especially impressive. A relatively small, two story building. Very ordinary. Except for the landscaping. It was sensational and included one large row of bushes sculpted to read National American Landscaping. Now, I thought, that's branding with a flourish.

Do I have too much time on my hands? That's a question I had begun asking myself. I was also asking myself why am I doing this? Fred Haller's gone. Probably dead at worst. Or, perhaps stashed as a John Doe in a mental ward in one of the 48 contiguous states at best. I take it back. That could even be worse than dead. I had to accept the fact that at some preternatural level I was becoming, if not consumed, then at least preoccupied with a matter I know I had created out of whole cloth. I decided, therefore, to drag the old bones over to the National American Landscape and ask a few questions. Would they accept an application from an octogenarian franchisee? Time to find out.

I drove over to the corporate office and found myself standing in front of a reception desk manned...what does one say and remain politically correct...womaned...womanized... by well, a woman? She was young, attractive except for what appeared to be a cud-like wad of gum getting a major league workout behind the reddest lips I had ever seen. She was a symphony of color. A mismatch with her bottled carrot colored hair framed by something purplish on both sides. Her skirt and blouse were nothing less than a symphony of color giving her the look of a gay pride flag. She asked what I wanted by raising her eyebrows.

"I'm interested in inquiring about a franchise." I said.

She brought the mastication to a halt. "Okay," she said, and pulled some papers from somewhere on the desk. "We have some forms for you to fill out. It's like an application." She smiled as if she were expecting a reward for her help.

"Thanks. But before I fill anything out I'd like to talk to someone about it. I have a lot of questions. Isn't there someone in management I can talk to first?"

"I'll see if Mr. Furman is in. He's a vice president for operations."

"Sounds like the right person to me." I gave her my name.

"Go ahead and fill out the forms and I'll see if he'll see you."

I took the paperwork to a couch on the other side of the room. She picked up a phone and resumed her attack on the gum. I pretended to study the paperwork and theatrically pulled out a pen as if I were actually going to fill out the application.

A few minutes later, she tapped on her desk to get my attention and told me Mr. Furman could indeed see me. She asked for the forms. I told her I'd bring them to Mr. Furman myself, that there were some things I wanted to go over with him first. She directed me to the stairs, apparently thought better of it and advised there was also an elevator. She said his office was the first door on the right when I got off.

Furman's allotted space was equipped with small reception office and a young woman who sat behind a small desk on which she had planted her elbows as if she were guarding the door behind her. "I'm Trav McGee here to see Mr. Furman. Are you his secretary?"

She was one of those Marian the Librarian types...brown hair pulled into a tight bun, big glasses, a dark pants suit. The thought flashed through my mind that with the glasses off, the hair let loose, and a more stylish outfit, she'd be a knockout. Why was she hiding herself?

"I'm his executive assistant," she corrected coolly puncturing my brief thought bubble. "Just this way," she said relinquishing her turf with a gesture, sweeping her arm toward the door like Vanna White when revealing the puzzle's answer. She left opening the door to me, allowing me the pleasure of meeting Mr. Furman.

He barely qualified as a "mister." I would have had no trouble calling him "sonny." He looked to be about twenty-five years old and he was scrambling into a suit coat as I stepped in. "Hello Mr. McRee," he said offering his hand after winning the wrestling match with the left sleeve of the coat. He wore horn rimmed glasses and a repp tie. Very Brooks Brothers.

"It's McGee," I corrected. "Tom McGee." He nodded his apology.

"I'm Mark Furman." He asked me to sit down. I did. So did he.

"I gather you are interested in joining the family."

I immediately disliked him. That "family" approach just does not work with me. "No, but I am interested in a possible franchise opportunity." I smiled at my little joke.

After a brief look of bewilderment, he did too. "Of course," he said.

"May I see your application forms?" I handed the papers to him.

"Oh, I thought you had filled them out. These

are blank."

"I wanted to learn more about what's involved before going through all of that. What does it take to set something up?"

He began a monologue that focused on investment. I was astonished that all it would take for me to join "the family" was a ten thousand dollar franchise fee, and bank confirmation that I could handle start up expenses and so on. The company would be behind me with its brand, training, management consultation, advertising, and would get a generous piece of the action.

He wanted to know if I were interested in something local or in joining the "family" in another part of the country. He was recommending another locale because "We pretty much have this area saturated...covered."

He took off his glasses indicating he was going to be very, very earnest. I couldn't wait.

"Forgive me for saying this Mr. McGee, but you're no teenager." He smiled sympathetically as a funeral director might at a mourning widow.

I chuckled. "I didn't think you'd notice."

"May I call you Tom?" he asked. I was beginning to think this guy was better at all of this than I thought when I first entered the office.

I nodded. "Sure. But most people call me Trav." He looked confused but accepted my allonym.

"I mention it because entering into one of our contracts requires a... shall we call it...long term commitment. He put his hands together and tapped his fingertips. I recognized the body language.

"Look, I'm eighty. Not a good age for long term commitments. But I'm interested in a franchise for one of my kids. He majored in horticulture at the university. I thought this might be a good thing for him. I've got the money to handle anything you can throw my way."

He smiled and stopped the finger tapping. The glasses went back on and he began rubbing his hands together as if he were sitting down to his favorite meal. After my assurances that I was financially solvent, I felt a little like that's what I was.

"One question I have though," and tried to act like this deal was just about signed, sealed and delivered, "is labor. Workers. Do you folks help at all with that?" I tried to look as if this were the most serious part of any potential transaction. "You just can't go to some street corner and find competent people. I know planting flowers is not rocket science, but it would be nice to have workers who know what they're doing. And, Mr. Furman," I winked at him, "we'd want good workers but not expensive good workers. Know what I mean?"

His smile broadened. "Oh, I know what you mean all right. And, that's another one of our services. We have a direct pipeline to the best workers around. Mexicans, Guatemalans, Hondurans, all looking for work. It's like a regular United Nations in this business. If you can't find them, we can fix you up."

Again, he removed his glasses. He took a tissue from a dispenser on his desk. He wiped one lens, then the other. Gradually, the preppy look disappeared and his features hardened. He no longer looked twenty something. He looked at me very seriously. "We can fix you up," he repeated, "for a price." He was Kaa the snake in Jungle Book.

"I understand. Just exactly how do you do that?" I leaned toward him, trying to convey the impression of a hand on the checkbook client.

The glasses went back on. The fingertip tap dance resumed. "The Hispanics are very good at this kind of work. Americans love, and almost demand, having spics crawling around their lawns and gardens. We've got operations over a big part of the country. Seasons change. It's seasonal work. We have a lot of workers at our disposal and we can move them around. They're good workers. Reliable. They know what they're doing. A lot of our people are not interested in taking chances on ex-cons, druggies or blacks. They like the little brown men." He showed me Kaa again. He thought his little soliloquy was pretty good.

I wanted to punch his preppy face, and spill a little blood on his Brooks Brothers suit. Here was a guy who was doing more than okay thanks, in large part, to "little brown men." I wondered if he realized that for many, if not most of these "little brown men" life was a desperate struggle of too little money, family separation, constant fear of being shuttled back to whatever and wherever it was that brought them north.

I had difficulty keeping my temper in check. "I gotta tell you I don't like that kind of talk."

"You will when they start making you money."

"Do they work for you, or would they work for me?"

"Both," he said. "We would have an arrangement."

"Sounds...what shall I say...financial. What kind of an arrangement? How much?"

"Everything's financial," he replied with a touch of condescension that put me off even further. I wondered what happened to the kid I met when I entered the office? He was gone, replaced by someone colder and tougher than I might have guessed half an hour earlier.

"How much? Sign the papers, come up with the fee, and we'll go from there." There was a real take it or leave it tone to his voice.

I couldn't believe we had gone this far in the conversation. On the one hand I welcomed his willingness to say so much to a stranger. On the other I was more than dismayed that someone like this...a company like this...was operating under the radar in my town. How to put it on the radar screen was the question.

I thanked Mark. Told him I'd talk it over with

the kids, and get back to him. I was happy to leave, in more ways than one.

"What do you think I should do now?" It was a question I put to Jeff when we met for one of our afternoon galas at Nellies. I had explained the details of my conversation with Furman. He listened with eyes wide under the snowy brows, and a jaw that dropped by degrees as I spoke. When I finished, he rubbed his chin and was silent for what seemed a long time.

"You know when you mentioned your theory the other day, I thought it was a little over the top. Actually, a lot over the top. Now, I'm not so sure. Now it makes more sense. I think." He shook his head from side to side. "I'd rather not believe something like that goes on. But these days..." his voice trailed off.

"There's another side to it too Trav.

"What's that?"

"If they are moving Mexicans, or whatever, around. Is that a bad thing? With all the crap that's been going on at the border, there are a lot of desperate people out there. All they want to do is work. They send billions back home giving their families a better life. Some come in on limited special guest worker visas, mostly to work in the fields. They're essential to growers all over the country. When the picking, sorting and cleaning work is done, some of them then drift into the shadows looking for other work.

"Others sneak across the border looking for work and a better life. You've seen all that on TV. Poor and desperate and running from bad ass druggies back home. If they aren't tossed back...the kids put in cages or whatever... and they make it through, then maybe they have a shot at a better life. You could make an argument that out-fits like the landscape people at least give them work and a few bucks to rub together and send home."

"Yeah, sounds like a very few bucks."

"Actually it's billions a year...and they pay taxes, but get zero benefits like Medicaid. But at least they have a life...maybe even a future. Blow up the process and what happens then? It's back to Nowheresville. What's worse?"

"So, what should I do?"

"I'm not sure you should do anything. On the one hand they can have something like a life. But, if you're right and think this outfit is trafficking in laborers...Hispanics...and that Fred Haller got a lit-tle too close for comfort, then this can be a very nasty game."

He gave me a very serious look. "We're just talking about men. Most of them cross alone. But some have women and kids in tow. I wonder what kind of work your friend Furman finds for them? Trafficking comes in all sizes, shapes and colors. And, by the way, you're too old for this sort of thing." He wagged a finger in admonition. Nellie thought it was a signal to bring another round. I was still thinking it over when she delivered.

"You could go to the authorities," Jeff said.

"I could. And they could think I was crazy."

"Maybe you are. And maybe you aren't." We sat in silence reflecting on the options.

"I think I'll get some advice from an expert," I eventually said.

"Who's that?"

"A cop friend."

I don't know if Paul Ansini was trying to dodge me or was busy, but it took me two days to finally reach him and another before he finally granted me an audience. It was kind of like that. I was a vassal petitioning royalty.

He was clearly not in the mood for a long conversation. I guess he was tired of our dialoguing over Fred Haller. I had told him over the phone that I had something he might want to know about.

"Haller again?" He asked.

"Sort of," I told him.

So, when I showed up at his office I had the distinct feeling he was prepared to make it a quick visit. He confirmed it when he said, "five minutes" before both feet where through the door.

I went through the story as quickly as I could and he listened with what I assumed was feigned interest. When I finished we resumed an old dialogue.

"Look McGee. You are way out of your element here. This isn't blowing the lid on a press secretary dealing drugs. Mark Furman is a good corporate citizen. He runs a good company."

"That kid runs the company? I thought he was a vice president or something."

"There are two Mark Furmans...senior and junior. Senior's teaching the kid the ropes."

"Ah...all in the family."

"Look, sticking your nose into the Haller case is one thing. That's a missing person case that we have investigated in a very professional way. It is ice cold, but still open. But thinking that a reputable company is trafficking laborers is way over the top. Like Haller, leave it to us.

"Look, if Furman has a few illegals on the payroll I'm not going to sweat it. I feel sorry for those folks. If they rape somebody or wave a gun at the local convenience store, that's one thing...I'm in. Making a buck is another. Go back to Nellie's, have a beer and take up backgammon or something."

I gave it one last shot. "And if there is trafficking?"

"McGee...you are not a good listener." He was clearly angry. "Go find something else to do. And, don't let the door hit you on the way out."

The "audience" was over.

That's why the phone call from Ansini was so surprising. It came the following evening. I graduate from beer to Boodles when the sun goes down and avoid the beer altogether unless I'm with Jeff. He was busy with something or other so my afternoon had been dry.

"I'm sorry I was short with you yesterday." That came before a hello and it took me a second or two to realize who was on the line.

"Detective Ansini?"

"Yeah. Look, I've been up to my gonads in a case I'm working. So worrying about a little undocumented workers is way off my radar. But I was listening to you."

I put down my Boodles as he continued.

"I got to thinking about what you had to say, and talked to some federal people I know. Furman's squeaky clean. An occasional illegal may be on the payroll from time to time, but it's no big deal. A look-the-other-way kind of thing from the feds. They also have bigger fish to fry." He paused.

"I tell you what. If anything breaks on the Haller case, I'll tell you. Hell, I'll tell you before her. All I ask is that you cool your jets. Don't play investigator. Taxpayers pay good money for people like me to do that kind of work." I did not respond.

"Okay? Deal?"

I felt like an eighth grader. "Okay Detective Ansini." I was embarrassed. "I didn't want to be involved with the whole Haller thing from the get-go. You're right," I mumbled,

"It won't be backgammon, but maybe I'll take up golf."

"Good boy," he said, now making me feel like a fourth grader.

Bowed and broken, I slithered out of the room.

In the following days I was feeling somewhat liberated. However, my back is killing me. My edema is not responding to diuretics, and my car needs a new clutch. First the battery now this. The car's falling apart too, but it's only ten year's old so I guess that should make me feel better. But it doesn't. Nor do the doctors. I've been in and out of specialists' offices for the past several days. Medicare's a godsend, but co-pays are piling up. They say getting old isn't for sissies. Getting old was not the problem. The problem is *being* old.

So it was when I received a phone call from Mary. Damn...isn't that behind me yet?

"Are we still friends?" I recognized her voice.

"Don't people say hello any more?"

"Trav, I'm sorry. I've been feeling guilty about asking you to get involved in Fred's disappearance. I know you tried to help. I'd like to make it up to you. Why don't you come over for dinner?" There was a pause, but before I could respond. "No talk about Fred."

That was good enough for me. "Sure Mary. I'd

love to."

"Bring your friend if you like."

"Jeff?"

"Yeah. I'd like to meet him. How about tomorrow night around six-thirty?"

"Deal," I said. "I'll let you know if Jeff can't make it. I'm guessing he will."

He could and we did.

It was a nice evening. Lots of chit-chat, reminiscing. After dinner, we sat in Mary's living room. We got on the subject of television. Mary and I had been in the business but admitted we didn't watch much local television news any more. Too much crime news. Jeff agreed.

We talked about growing up with radio, Sky King, Tom Mix, the Shadow, Lone Ranger and listening to afternoon soap operas when we were home sick from school.

Jeff said how much he used to enjoy Amos and Andy, two black men played by white creators.

"Television killed them," he said. "The radio program was really good, but they made the characters clowns on TV. It was dreadful and had a short run in the fifties. The stereotypes did not play well about the time the Supreme Court was deciding Brown versus the Board of Education. The modern civil rights era was off and running."

I had done some research on the program for

a series I wanted to do in my television days. The news director and general manager spiked it as potentially too controversial. I knew that the program ran for thousands of episodes. For fifteen years starting in the late twenties it ran six nights a week and was listened to by multiple millions of people every night. It moved to one night a week during the war, and was on the air for more than a decade after that until it too made people uncomfortable in the fifties. The radio broadcasts ended about the same time as the TV series.

"A lot of white people listened and loved the characters. It would never get on the air today on radio or television," I said.

We remembered the quiz shows and evening dramas which were so popular until television, top 40 music and rock and roll blew them away like so much dust.

Conversation eventually waned. Jeff being Jeff joined Mary in the kitchen to help with the dishes. I wandered around the living room and took another tour of the crammed book shelves. I noticed that the books on photography were gone.

I saw an old John le Carré best seller I had never read. And wandered into the kitchen interrupting what seemed a cozy conversation. I asked Mary if I could borrow the book. She said I could have it, that she was trying to de-clutter and that most of the books would be among the first things to go.

"Yeah, I noticed that those nice books on

photography are gone," I said.

"Yes they are. A friend wanted them. I was happy to give them to her."

Jeff said, "Well, if you're wanting to get rid of some books, I'll take a look too if you don't mind?" She nodded. He wiped his hands on a towel, handed it to me, and went into the living room.

"I guess I have a job," I said, picking up a service plate.

"Thanks again for dinner Mary. It was delicious."

"And, thank you again Trav. I'm sorry I brought you into my anxious world and my grief. I appreciate your trying to help."

A moment later, Jeff returned with an arm full of books, including the one I wanted. I told him I had first dibs on it, he handed it to me, we chatted for a few more minutes before repeating our thanks to Mary and left.

"You two seemed to get along well," I said as we walked to my car. "Do I see a romance in your future?" I teased.

He chuckled. "No sir, you don't. She's actually thinking about moving to Florida to live with an old widow friend from school. And," he added, "old Fred's still got her heart." A few steps later he added, "I also think she could use the money from selling the house."

We reached my car. "I might have to sell my condo if this old wagon needs any more work."

I opened the door for him. "Hop in. And don't try to leave with that le Carré book."

"I didn't know you were into John le Carré," he said. "I thought you were all about Amos and Andy."

"Jeff," I said, "hop in."

It was not someone I expected to hear from given the tone of our last meeting in which I was at least semi-humiliated. But there was Detective Paul Ansini on the other end of an eight a.m. phone call. It was a Saturday and my day had been getting off to a lazy start.

"I'm a man of my word," he said. "We found a body...It could be Fred Haller."

I was not expecting that. "Wow! Where? When?"

He gave me the CliffsNotes version. It was pretty much a scenario a lot of people had probably expected. Certainly one Ansini had thought to be among the possibilities.

A hunter had stumbled across the remains in a heavily wooded area some twenty miles from the city. He was hunting without a permit and had found the body a few days earlier. He didn't report it at first, afraid that he would get into trouble for poaching. But, his conscience got the best of him and he finally called it in.

"Have you contacted Mary Haller?" I asked.

"Nope. We want to make sure it's him first."

"How do you do that? He's been out there a long time."

"We'll eyeball him. Then do the DNA thing." He added, "I'm heading out there now to get the ball rolling."

"I'd like to come with you?"

"I thought you might want to. It's not in the rule book. You can come if you keep it to yourself and keep out of the way when we get there. I'll tell folks you're a reporter for that magazine you're with." He paused then asked, "Who are you writing for?"

"You're my new best friend," I said, dodging the question and feeling guilty because I had made up the business about doing a story.

He ignored the comment. "You're on my way," he said. I'll pick you up in five minutes." Click.

If nothing else, Detective Ansini was on a five minute clock for just about everything.

It was a pretty day for a drive anywhere, especially through rural countryside. The sun was bright and warm reflecting what remained of the dew in roadside fields. There was a cloudless blue high sky. It was the kind of sky that caused good outfielders to flip their sunglasses when chasing line drives. When we reached a heavily wooded area dappled trees and bushes seemed more vibrantly green than normal. Shades and shadows, shadows and shades.

Driving with Ansini was something well south of a gabfest. Clearly he had this matter on his mind and was not in a mood to bond. There was a lot of chatter on his radio, most of which was unintelligible to me. He would respond from time to time speaking mostly in numbers.

I was as eager as he was to get to the site. Crime was not my beat in the TV days so I knew I was opening a door to a room I did not know.

Thanks to GPS, and a friendly lady whose voice sounded like a girlfriend from long, long ago, we found the spot we were guided to. It was not Route 66, but a rutted path in a field near the woods. And while I had not known what to expect, the scene was one I had seen dozens of times on television crime dramas. Officers waiting around. A crime scene in the offing.

There were two highway patrol cars and a sheriff's van parked with engines running and lights flashing. They were adjacent to what appeared to be an overgrown path leading into a heavily wooded area. One officer was standing by his vehicle and on his radio. A bearded, farmer type, wearing an OshKosh ensemble and a John Deere cap, stood away from both cars looking a lot like he didn't want to be there. I assumed he was the guy who discovered the body.

"State's got the scene along with the sheriff's office," said Ansini as we made our way toward the vehicles. "I'm just along for the ride until we find out if he...the body...belongs to the city. It's a juris-dictional thing."

He touched my arm. "Remember what I said...stay out of the way and keep quiet." He looked at me like a man who meant what he said.

I did just that as he approached the patrol offi-cer, showed his badge and chatted. When the offi-cer pointed to what had appeared to be the path into the heavily shaded copse of brush and trees, Ansini signaled me and I followed him into the darkness.

Television doesn't do it justice. It never looks as bad on the screen as it really is. And, this was a bad scene. A couple of deputies and a highway pa-trol officer were standing and talking near a large black rubber tarp. It didn't take much imagin-ation to figure out what was beneath it. Ansini approached. I followed him for a step or two, then held back not certain I wanted or needed to be any closer, and pretty sure Ansini meant it when told me not to "get in the way."

The detective exchanged a few words with the other officers, when one of the deputies pulled back the tarp about half way. Another exchange of words and the deputy pulled back all the way. I was close enough to see what was beneath the covering. I was reminded of another Travis McGee line..."Never sit in the first row at the ballet."

It was not a pretty picture though it took me a

moment to put it all together. My first impression was of a few bits and pieces of cloth until I focused in on bones... clearly human detritus. And flies swooping in and around the debris. Ansini told me later that like kids at a birthday party, they never want to leave after the cake and ice cream are gone.

Ansini gestured to pull the covering all the way down. A human skull was at one end of the pile. Bits of darkened skin clung to bone. Fragments of hair were visible even from where I was standing. It was not an intact skeleton for other bones were scattered for a few feet in all directions. I knew enough to know that woodland critters had gotten to the corpse. The bones had been dispersed as tiny, and perhaps some larger animals had ravaged the body. The bones were like pieces of a puzzle tossed on a table. They had been picked clean.

It was hard to imagine that what was left on the ground had once been a living, thinking, breathing human being. Aside from some obviously recognizable pieces like the skull and pelvis it would have been difficult to identify them as human remains at all. The question now was whether what lay before us was Fred Haller. And if not, who was it?

Ansini spent several minutes poking around the debris, careful not to move anything beyond where the remains had already been scattered. From time to time, he would confer with the other men, then return to his prodding. After about twenty minutes of this, he wiped his hands as if he were washing them and returned to me.

"Well?" I asked.

"Can't tell much given the state of the remains, but I'm guessing it's not Haller. Bits of pieces of clothing don't match what he was wearing the last time his wife saw him. Hard to tell size because of the way the bones have been scattered. The body hasn't been there for a year. Maybe six months."

"But," I said, "It's possible he didn't walk out of the house, into the woods, and die. He could have been staying someplace for weeks or months. or been wearing different clothes...if it's Haller."

"True enough." Ansini turned back toward the scene just as the other officers were recovering the remains with the black rubber shroud.

"But does that really make sense to you Trav?"

"Not really I guess." I noted that was the first time Ansini had ever used my first name. "What now?"

"Let's get out of here," he said as he began walking back to his car.

"The boys out here have custody of the body. It's their investigation. All they can do now is wait for forensics and to get the remains packed up. They'll try to determine if there was any foul play."

He chuckled. "Fat chance of that given what's left of whoever it is...was." We got to the car. He turned to me.

"The tough part for me now is having to go to

the little woman, explain what we found and..."

"And?"

"And see if she's got something around we can use to make a DNA identification. We gotta do it. We have a missing person and a body. We've got to determine if the body is our missing person. I don't think it is, but we have to go through the motions."

"Jeez. That's going to be tough on Mary."

"That's why you're going to do it."

"What? Me? Why me?"

"Because I'm busy and you're her friend. You can give her some love at the same time."

I shook my head. "Hey, it's your job. If there're any questions she has...and she will have questions...you're the one to answer them." I was pissed off and flummoxed. "And, isn't there something called chain of custody or chain of evidence? You can't just pass evidence around."

"Don't worry about it. It's not that kind of evidence. We just need an old toothbrush or something. And I'll bet you're good at making nice." By then he was sitting in the driver's seat.

As I got in, he said, "It's Saturday. It'll take a couple of days to get the answers. The yokels out here aren't the swiftest."

"Ansini, as they say, this ain't right." I slammed the car door.

"It wasn't right when I invited you to drive out here with me either. But I did, and you agreed."

Check mate I thought shaking my head, grudgingly agreeing to contact Mary. I was not looking forward to it. But I did learn something about one Detective Paul Ansini that could be useful. He was a good cop who played by the book...except when he didn't. He took me to the scene when he probably should not have. He was asking me to do something he should have done. I stashed that tidbit in the old memory bank hedging my bet when it came to Detective Ansini. My memory wasn't always what it once was, but I didn't think I'd have any problem remembering that.

I didn't have it in me to call Mary when I got back to my place. I knew I'd have to get whatever she might find to give me over the weekend so it would be ready to go under the microscope on Monday.

It was early in the afternoon, and a storm was blowing in. The sky was dark enough for me to have to turn on the lights. It was too cozy inside to think about trying to find something to do outside. So I decided to learn more about DNA.

I had no idea what's involved. What should Mary and I be looking for. Ansini had mentioned a tooth brush. Really. I had heard about cheek swabs, semen and hair. But I was surprised to learn that skin cells from just about any source, including fingerprints can be tested, and that under certain conditions it can even be derived from footprints.

The DNA in our bodies can last for hundreds, even millions of years. That had the remains in the woods covered, but what about what Fred might have left behind at the house? No saliva, no fingernail clippings, no skin scrapings, and probably no tooth brush.

And it seems DNA testing from typical sources was not always reliable. Exposure to sunlight, moisture and other elements can degrade it. A toothbrush not used for a long time might not be a reliable source. I thought I'd have to mention that to my favorite detective the next time I saw him. It seemed to me that the best source would be Fred's hair. And, without Fred, as difficult to get as cheek swabs.

What then? The actual testing was obviously not in my hands. Good thing. I assumed that whatever was being analyzed would be put in a test tube with some chemical, shaken a few times then observed through a microscope. It is a lot more sophisticated than that and it made me understand why I was never captain of the science team. The process includes four steps called extraction, quantitation, amplification, and capillary electrophoresis. Yada, yada, yada. That's where I stopped my "research." My interest level was high, but my understanding of such scientific jargon was not a good match.

I decided I'd call Mary in the morning, and fell sleep waiting for Saturday Night Live. It isn't funny anymore anyway. Not like the old days with Dan Aykroyd, Gilda Radner and Phil Hartman.

So instead of looking for laughs I fell asleep hoping we could find a few of Fred's hairs.

I called mid-morning but there was no answer. I assumed she was at church although I had never thought of her as much of a churchgoer. Maybe Fred's disappearance has changed her, I thought.

I didn't have much stock with the church myself. Under parental decree I sang in a church choir as a kid. The voice change at age twelve or so ended that chapter in my life. But I had heard so many boring sermons delivered by a pompous and colorless Episcopal priest I swore off, much comforted by a lifelong religious abstinence with the words of my hero Travis McGee..."Organized religion is like being marched in formation to watch the sunset." No wonder I love the guy.

I did catch Mary early in the afternoon and was surprised to learn that she had been out for coffee with...wait for it...Jenny Hacker, her next door neighbor. That one caught me off guard. I had no idea that relationship included anything but animosity. But, who knows about such things?

I told her I had something I needed to talk about and that I'd like to drop by. She seemed slightly hesitant but said I should come by sooner rather than later, that she had plans for the evening. For Mary, obviously, life was moving on.

I arrived an hour or so later. She looked as relaxed as she had when we worked together. She even had a little color going...in her complexion and in her pretty dress. It made me all the more uneasy about this mission. She looked like time was marching on and had erased some of the anxiety over Fred's departure. I worried that my news could prompt a relapse of who knows what consequence?

"Mary," I said after she brought coffee, "there's some news." I was speaking softly and, I hoped, with what she would understand as compassion.

"About Fred?" she asked with a start as she brought a hand to her throat.

"Possibly."

She sat silently with an understandably quizzical expression.

"They have found a body," I said.

"Oh my god!" Her hands went to her cheeks that suddenly flared red.

I waited before continuing, expecting tears that never came.

"Mary...you have to know that they don't know for certain. It's a badly decomposed body of a man found in the woods about twenty miles from here. There's not much left but bones."

She gasped.

"For a positive identification they need a DNA sample."

Her hands dropped to her lap. Still no tears. She looked at me in a manner I could not translate. Was it resentment because of what I was telling her, or an inner strength; a resolve to work through this news? I couldn't tell. I waited for some clear response.

"Like what?" she finally said.

"They need a sample of his cells," I said simply. "Something he left behind they can match with the DNA of...of what they found in the woods."

There was a long pause as she digested what I had said.

"Ansini says it could be something as simple as a tooth brush." I paused. "Hair's best. Fingernail clippings better," I smiled hoping she'd realize it was, and was not, a joke.

She looked at me with a strange, questioning expression. It was not the crack about fingernail clippings she was responding to. It was the detective's name.

"Ansini? Detective Ansini. You've been talking to him?"

"Mary. I was with him when he went out to examine the body site. He asked me to talk to you about all of this. He thought it would be easier on you if it were quote, a less official visit, unquote."

She kneaded her hands. "When did you find this...body?"

"Yesterday."

"So you've sat on this for a full day without

telling me?"

"Yes Mary. They can't do a DNA test until tomorrow. We wanted to leave as little time as possible between letting you know and starting the tests, so that you wouldn't have to wait so long between hearing the news and getting a result."

She nodded, apparently accepting the rationale. She got up and turned as if to leave the room. "Stay here. I'll see what I can find." She left the room, leaving me wishing that it was Ansini, and not I who had brought this news to Mary Haller. As I watched her leave the room I wondered if I could have handled it as well as she did under the same circumstances. I thought back to the moments after learning of Jennifer's death and I knew I could not have.

I waited, wishing I had a Boodles in hand. This had not been a pleasant experience for me. I wandered around the living room eager for Mary's return. It took less time than I might have expected. She returned in about twenty minutes with a paper bag. It seemed full.

"Okay, I found some things. I guess it was a good thing that I just couldn't bring myself to send it all to the Good Will. No fingernail clippings," she said with a trace of a smile, letting me know she got the attempt at humor.

"There are a couple of sweaters. Maybe some hairs on them. Maybe some Dandruff. That works too, I think. And, a hair brush. And...a toothbrush.

God knows why I kept that. I guess these are things you can work with."

"Not me Mary. Not me. This goes to the world of twenty-first century science. Not to a broken down reporter." I smiled in what I hoped she would accept as an apologetic gesture. "I didn't want to do this."

"I know," she said. "I know. Let me get you a drink."

I felt better already. "I'd love one."

"I think I'll have one too," she said.

We sat and talked about next steps and timing and I assured her that what I knew about DNA tests indicated that we should have some information within a couple days at best...a week or two at most.

I said, "I have to be sure you know that the tests may not be conclusive."

"In a funny way," she said. "I hope it's Fred. Then again, I really hope it's not and that he's out there somewhere. Like the song 'Somewhere Out There'. Remember that? Linda Ronstadt. From an animated movie, but very pretty." For a moment she looked as if she were a million miles away. "Fred and I loved Linda Ronstadt."

"Me too," I said. "Pretty and talented."

"You've got to stop calling women pretty," she said. "It can get you in trouble."

"Hah. Don't I know it."

"Now, you've got to get out of here. I have a dinner date."

"Good for you. Who's the lucky guy?"

"Gal," she said. "My new best friend, Jenny Hacker."

"Whoa. A twofer...coffee and dinner? I'm surprised. I thought they, or you, would be building a wall between your places."

"Ah, that was Fred and Mark. Jenny almost ran me down the other day in that big red rocket of hers. She apologized. We talked. She's not so bad. She's going into business for herself."

"Hah. That's interesting. Careful. She'll try and sell you a million dollar condo."

"I'll settle for her selling this place."

"Really? You thinking of moving?"

"Maybe. Her business plan's interesting. Different. Guaranteed sale. If she can't sell it, she'll buy it. I can use the bucks. I want to do some things before I die," she said wistfully. "A little travel. A smaller place. Away from the memories. I have been pretty much tied to right here since Fred...." She couldn't finish, but I understood.

I did wish I could be a fly on the wall for that get together with Jenny. "A change of scenery might do you good," I said.

She finished her drink. "I did take a couple of short trips to visit friends in Florida a while back, but I don't feel right leaving with all the uncertainty," adding, "and money's a little short." She offered a smile that didn't quite make it.

I felt I had an instinct and understanding for Jenny's "business plan." I could imagine her harvesting listings of middle and upper middle class homes, be something less than energized about selling them, then gobble them up herself for a price well under top dollar, then flip them for a tidy profit. Pocket change when the million dollar market sagged. I did not share that thought with Mary. She'd received enough incoming for one day. "Mary. I'm out of here. Enjoy your dinner. Give my best to the Hackers." I hoped I sounded sincere.

I brought the bag Mary had given me to Ansini the following morning. He was in but busy and we had no more time together than it took for him to say thanks and ask how Mary took the news and request. I told him it was not as bad as I thought it might have been and that I thought time was doing what it does about healing wounds. She wasn't there yet I told him, but getting there to the point of thinking about moving away. He raised his eyebrows.

"Yeah. She apparently went to Florida for a couple of days. And to Europe on one of those river cruises. She told me before she left each time and gave me ways to get in touch with her." He shrugged his shoulders. "I never had to, obviously. She called me first thing when she got back to check in."

The Europe trip was a surprise to me. She'd never mentioned it to me. Not that she should have. But, those trips are expensive and I knew she was on a tight budget. Good for her that she could pull it off I thought.

The testing he told me could be completed in as little as a day or two, or as long as two weeks. He was not confident that the out of town labs could or would work quickly on the tests. He told me he'd let me know.

"Who gets to tell Mary if that corpse is or is not Fred?"

"If it's Fred, you do. If not, I do."

"You know Ansini, you're a bit of a prick."

"Only kidding. But I'd like you to go with me whatever way it goes."

"Why?"

"Just because. I gotta go."

The following two days were filled with the usual activities of an octogenarian. I had two doctor's appointments. One for the nagging edema problem which continued to stump my cardiologist, the other the annual check up with my eye doctor...an ophthalmologist with a mission...cataract surgery. I thought it could wait. He was disappointed.

It was Thursday that Ansini called. He told me the remains in the woods were not those of Fred Haller. DNA tests confirmed that at just about the time the local law enforcement people had gone through their old files and had a ten month missing person case most had forgotten about. A woman. Her husband had reported her missing…an apparent dementia case. And, it turned out to be a murder.

He told me the story. "They went to her husband to get some DNA samples for a test. When the results came up with a match, they went to tell him. They found him on a couch, drunk almost senseless. He'd been drinking for a couple of days. Apparently he was on a pretty big guilt trip and felt it was only a matter of time before the sheriff put it all together.

"When he sobered up he broke down and just blurted out that he'd killed her. Seems he had just had enough of the little woman and did her in with a knife."

"Right out of the movies," I said.

He went on. He obviously enjoyed telling the story. "Given the shape the body was in he probably could have gotten away with the original story. They lived alone. There was no one to say that she hadn't gone gaga."

"You do have a way with words, Ansini.

"Crime does not pay," he said, and I could hear the smile in his voice. "Crime does not pay."

"I'll remember that the next time I plan to commit one. Back to the beginning. What now? You tell Mary yet?"

"No. I just got the report. You want to do it? It's good news, not like the last time."

"No, I think this needs an official touch. You do it. Alone. I'm opting out."

There was a long pause. He exhaled loudly. "Okay. No problem. See you around."

I hung up wondering why a veteran detective, a tough guy, was so reluctant to interact with someone like Mary. It was a question for another day, if there were another day with him. But, of course, the Fred Haller case was back to square one. He was still missing.

The same unanswered questions remained. I felt for Mary. She had told me she really hoped that the body in the woods was Fred and that that would end it and she could get him his marker, and get on with her life.

ANSINI

I could never tell McGee that he has helped me in my work. At least not yet. He was a pain in the ass when he first came in, wanting my help in what seemed to be a hopeless case of finding a guy who disappeared months ago. He's dead. I know he's dead. That's the way these things work. He's an old guy. He didn't run away with some broad. He isn't a patient in some state hospital someplace. If he were, our inquiries would have produced something. He's dead!

My guess is Alzheimer's. He wandered off. Got lost. Fell. Maybe into a creek or river. One of these days, we'll get something on it. Maybe not. I really thought we had something when that body was found in the woods. That's the way it'll happen. Someone will find a body. It'll be Haller. Meantime, McGee can keep Miss Mary happy and keep her out of my hair. She's been a nuisance for a year. She's settled down a little bit lately, but I don't want to spend a lot of my time babysitting her. I'll leave that to McGee. I have bigger fish to fry. Thanks to McGee.

I'll tell her that the body was not her husband, and hope that she does move out of town like McGee said she was planning to do. Good riddance.

I don't mind talking to suspects, witnesses or victims, but I do not like talking to people who don't fall into any of these categories. Small talk is not my strong suit. I know it. To me, it's a waste of time. That's why I wanted to go "over and out" with my conversation with Mary Haller.

The way I see it is that most of the people I deal with are bad people...people I distrust...and people I generally distrust...I dislike. I've seen too many so called good folks who turn out to be bad. Too much bad makes it difficult for me to deal well with people who are good. Where's McGee when I need him?

With Mary Haller it went better than I thought it might.

"Mary, it's good news." She was stoic when I told her that the body we'd found was not Fred's. You could have put her reaction among the faces on Mount Rushmore. Carved in rock. I expected emotion of some sort.

Mary had told me that she had a hope that it was Fred so that all of it could be over. I started to tell her the story about the victim and the murder, but she didn't want to hear it. I was disappointed. I thought it was fairly entertaining.

She thanked me for bringing me the news personally. And she made it clear that there was not much interest in further conversation. Fine by me. Like I say, I have bigger fish.

When McGee came into my office with questions about National American Landscaping, you could have dropped me. He was all wound up about an immigration problem. But I had stumbled onto something else. That name had popped up on my radar earlier. I thought it was an odd coincidence, or providence, that McGee has brought up the company and the Furmans.

I play hunches in my game. I decided to stir a pot. I think the Furman boys...upstanding citizens they are supposed to be...are up to their chinny chin chins in drugs. I'm trying to make that case. But I have to be careful. They are upstanding citizens according to the mayor and most of the members of the city council. Money buys that sort of thing. And, the Furmans have money. And they have a ready made network with their franchise operation.

Illegals in on it? Some probably. I think some of their franchise owners in this state, and others, could be in on it too. It would be quite a coup to bring something like that down. I need to do as much of it as I can on my own before bringing in the Narcotics dicks and having to give it all up to them.

I checked in with lieutenant in the Drug Enforcement Unit and asked if they had anything at all on Mark Furman and his dad and National American. Nothing. I said I was going to look into a tip and would do it on my own dime if they didn't mind my taking baby steps on their turf. That was no problem. They had plenty to keep them busy for a long time. Like most police operations, they were overworked and understaffed. Their world was a world of opioids, heroin and grass. Opioids, and their close cousin heroin, are killers...especially together. I promised I'd keep them in the loop and turn them on to anything I might come up with.

Young Mark Furman was the heir apparent at National American. Not too long out of college and a nice job with dad. But something didn't fit. I ran a records search on National American Life. It pinged on the company and his name came up in connection with a couple of busts. Nothing serious; A DUI and an assault complaint that won him a little court time and a few hundred in fines.

But his name was also coupled with some characters who did not match the silver spoon, preppy résumé. Some party girls, who partied for a living, and made a pretty good living at it...a guy arrested for assault bailed out by Furman...some teenagers looking to buy weed. His name floated around the edges. There was gossip in the hallways as there always is when people with prominent connections get into trouble. I had heard the name around headquarters. I didn't think much of it. He was young. He was connected.

Trouble usually came to me. I wasn't interested in going and looking for it. I had enough on my plate. But McGee got me to thinking. And, I really got to thinking when Furman's name showed up on a brand new arrest report. Drunk and disorderly. He was still in the tank the day after the arrest. I was surprised he hadn't been bailed out. I decided to pay him a visit and to pull some threads to see what, if anything would unravel.

The drunk tank is not a place anyone wants to be. Not drunk. Not sober. Not anything. It's a big common cell often filled with, you guessed it, drunks or druggies. They run the gamut from swells in tuxedos to young toughs in T-shirts and jeans. It's loud. Men shout obscenities. Grown men cry. Others try to sleep it off on hard wooden benches.

It smells like sweat and piss and vomit. Sometimes like blood. People come in bloody after being picked up for assault and brawls. And, because a lot of them are drunk and disorderly for a long time after they're arrested, fights break out, often resulting in broken teeth and broken other things too. More blood. And they stay that way for a long time until they're processed out. "Out" may just mean a move down the hall to a cleaner, smaller cell.

For some, the move, whatever it happens to be, happens fairly quickly in real time. The usual stay is eight to ten hours. That's a long time in an environment like that. Everyone wants out and wants out quickly. Mark Furman was no exception. He was dirty and sweaty and bloody. In other words he fit right in with a Thursday night crowd. For some reason Thursday nights are busy in the tank. Blame it on office happy hours and on getting a head start on Friday and Saturday partying.

I checked the report. He had been arrested for fighting in a dingy bar in an even dingier part of town. It was home away from home for all types, from pushers and perverts...from pimps and prostitutes...and every lowlife in between. It seemed pretty far off the Furman family's beaten path. He was drunk at the time of arrest and gave officers a "do you know who I am?" defense. That never works. They got him into a squad car without ceremony making sure his head got a good rap as they shoved him into the back seat. Twenty minutes later he was ensconced in the squalor of the tank keeping a wide berth from with his buddies licking their wounds on the other side of the big cell. There were plenty of other miserables there separating them, not that any of the belligerents seemed interested in continuing the war.

The interesting part to me was that the heavily tattooed guys Furman had gotten into the beef with were a far cry from the silver spoon crowd.

One was carrying. All were in possession of a variety of drugs, from grass to meth to opioid. All had arrived at the bar at the same time and probably together. All got drunk together. All was well, until all hell broke loose for whatever reason. So Mark Furman was slumming that Thursday night, and with some guys that definitely came from the other side of the moon, not his side. Or did they? Or did he? And, what was the problem?

I decided to pay him a visit.

I was directed to his office the following Monday morning by a colorful receptionist with funky hair. Furman was expecting me. I had called earlier and said I needed to talk to him about his arrest...just wrapping up details of the investigation. He was not enthusiastic about it, but agreed.

I was intrigued by the name Mark Furman. Sounded the same as the famous detective at the O.J. trial...the one who got all the publicity for finding lots of bloody and incriminating evidence the jury wouldn't buy. It was probably because he was quoted saying things that fit into the playbook of any card carrying racist. I had forgotten he spelled his name with an "h"...Fuhrman.

The trial took place about the time this young man would have been born. I wondered if this one's parents had a weird sense of humor. Or, perhaps had such a high regard for that Mark Fuhrman that they named their little Furman Mark? A question for another day.

He sat behind his desk wearing a crisp white shirt, a red and white striped tie, a blue blazer, and a shiner the size of a baseball blossoming behind his glasses. A red lump on his forehead matched his tie and completed the look of a guy who had come out second best in the barroom rumble. I thought of advice given me as a teenager; when you have zits, wear a distracting bright shirt.

He looked uncomfortable as I sat down. I knew he was embarrassed when he tried to make a predictable joke about his appearance. "I zigged when I should have zagged," he said with a phony chuckle. I almost expected him to add the equally predictable, "But you should see the other guy."

He must have known that I knew better.

"So, what's this all about Detective...Ansini is it?"

I nodded. "It's about that fracas in the bar the other night."

"Yeah, that was a bad scene. Got pretty rough there for a while." He looked at his hands as if examining his nails. He was not into eye contact. "It'll cost me a couple of bucks. I guess I can afford it. What's a couple of bucks."

Spoiled brat...entitled rich kid. Now I felt I knew the guy.

"I need to know a little more about the boys you were with." He continued focused on his hands. "There were some bad fellows you were

hanging with. One had a gun. They all face possession charges." I paused. "You too."

He was now focusing on something on the
wall across the room.

"Grass...some Fentanyl. What the hell was
going on?"

Finally, he looked in my direction. Not at me.
More like over my shoulder.

"I don't know. I hardly know them. I was at a
party. We were tossing them down..."

"Drugs?"

"No. Just shots. Jägermeister. Anyway, there
were other folks there. It got pretty loud, and one
of the guys suggested we take the party someplace
else. Seemed like a good idea at the time. So we did."
He shot his arms toward the ceiling, a great big
stretch.

"What started the fight?"

"Who knows. Somebody said something to
somebody else. All of a sudden fists were flying.
Next thing I know I'm on the receiving end, and
being shoved into a cop car."

He went on to complain about the tank and
being held there for so long. His father bailed him
out the next morning, making him wait good and
long before putting up the cash. Furman said his
dad wanted him to stew in his own juice. He was
totally pissed because it was an embarrassment to
the family and an embarrassment to the business.

He wanted sonny boy to learn a lesson. It was quite a weekend at home. I was surprised he still lived at home. A Boomeranger.

He told me how he apologized to his parents and promised to be a good boy and work harder than ever for good old National American Landscaping. He mentioned the company name in a way that made me think he was not all that fond of the family enterprise.

"In any case, a little fine, a slap in the wrist, and that'll be that," he said. "I really don't know what you're doing here. This doesn't seem like a very serious matter to me." He shuffled some papers on his desk. He was nervous and I thought probably smart enough to know that it was not SOP for a police detective to pop in to discuss a drunk and disorderly charge. Small beads of sweat glistened above his lips. I let him sweat. Sometimes if you don't say anything in a conversation like this, it's the best way to get the other party to talk whether they want to or not.

"Is it the drugs?" he asked. "I was clean. I didn't have any drugs. Pot doesn't really count anymore."

I waited several seconds. "Do you use?"

"No...no...I don't use. I may drink too much from time to time but I stay away from that hard stuff. Maybe an occasional joint" He began rubbing his chin. "Christ...don't bring that up with my father. He's freaked enough as it is."

"Well Furman...here's the thing. One of your

buddies is talking. And, he's talking about you. Want to know what he's saying?"

He didn't respond. Apparently done with the examination of his hands, and finished with rearranging his desktop paperwork, he finally looked directly at me with his eyes blinking nervously. He took a couple of deep swallows.

"He's telling us that everything he had on him he got from you. He says you guys go back a couple of years, and that you've been a pretty reliable source for just about anything anybody might need...from speed to...well you name it." He shook his head slowly. "Especially marijuana."

Now he was rubbing his hands and slowly they morphed into little fists.

"Now, I'm not a prude. Pot's not what it used to be. Doctors are prescribing it all over the country. Recreational use has become the new big thing. Not in this state, but a lot of states are coming 'round. So, I'm not going to worry too much about a little weed. Fentanyl. That's another story. It kills people, lots of them kids. Kills them dead! And anyone fucking around with it is looking at some serious shit."

I stopped right there as he sat back sharply in his chair as if he'd watched me run through a stoplight. Jaw muscles were dancing. I have to admit I do enjoy seeing little turds like Mark Furman squirm. And, he was doing a pretty good version of it at that moment. I loved it.

"I don't have anything to do with it. A little grass? Yeah. But that's all. I'm in the landscaping business after all." He tried to laugh but it came out as more of a choking sound.

"Very funny," I said. "But if I find out you've gone pharmaceutical... your ass is grass." He didn't think that was funny. I did.

"We're going after this in a big way," I said. "Too many people are dying. So, if you're even close to it on the sidelines, it's going to get nasty."

"I'm not into it," he said so softly I could barely hear him.

"What?"

"A little pot..." his voice trailed off.

"Where did these guys get the drugs. Any idea?"

He started digging his finger into his ear. An excavating job that was another turn off. He retrieved it. Examined the finger tip. He was taking his time with the answer.

"Nope. I don't go in for that stuff. A little pot now and then," he repeated, adding, "I stay away from the hard stuff."

Our eyes held each other in a standoff.

"Believe me."

As a cop, I have learned that when someone tells me to "believe me," I need to be convinced. And there was nothing in this conversation that convinced me that this young man was anything but a dickhead.

"I'll be in touch," I said standing to go. "Here's my card. If you think of anything you need to tell me, let me know." I turned toward the door. Before it closed behind me, I thought I heard the sound of a grown man weeping.

I was intercepted in the lobby by Mark Furman's father. He introduced himself as Mark senior, effectively ending my speculation about the O.J. detective. Senior was born long before O.J. Simpson ever played professional football, much less killed his wife, which I thought he did.

Mark Senior was an older version of the kid, right down to the glasses and the preppy tie. After the introductions, he called me off to the side of the lobby and a little private chat.

I didn't like this guy from the get-go. "What's this all about Ansini?" It really pissed me off when people I have just met call me by my last name. I do have a first name, and a title.

"I beg your pardon Mark." I put a nice sarcastic spin on it when I pronounced his name.

"My son. What did you need to see my son about?" His tone was demanding and his expression unfriendly bordering on outright hostile.

"Well Mark," I said making sure to use his first name again, "I think that's between me and him. He is over 21 right?" I gave him a big smile hoping he did not miss its insincerity.

He wasn't reading me. "I know he got himself

into a bit of a jam the other night. But I didn't think that would require a visit from a cop at our place of business."

"Well, it did. One of the guys he was arrested with was throwing some accusations around. If you want to know about it ask Junior. It's between me and him. If he wants it between the three of us, that's up to him."

"What kind of accusations?"

"Ask him." I gave him a fuck you look and headed for the door.

It's probably not a good idea for me to be saying this, but when I don't like people, or when they're disrespectful, and they appear to be on the wrong side of the law, I'm going to work a little harder to find out if they are or they aren't. And if they are, watch out!

I made it a point to catch up with a guy by the name of Gary Goodstrich. I didn't have far to go. He was one of those arrested along with Mark Furman after the barroom brawl. He was in trouble. He was still in custody and probably would be for a while.

When he was arrested, he had an unregistered gun, a couple of ounces of grass, and enough Fentanyl on him to fill a Pez dispenser. He had obviously gone out to party hard the night of the fight.

He was out of the tank, but was alone in a cell at the city jail. Compared to the tank, it was the

Hilton in spite of the steel bed and the open toilet and the no window. I was introduced to him there, and had arranged to chat with him in one of those little rooms where lawyers meet with clients. Not much better than the cell.

G.G., as he eventually told me he wanted to be called, looked the part of a tough guy, or someone who wanted to look tough. He was not a country club type and not exactly typecast as a best buddy for a Mark Furman type I thought.

G.G. had long hair, a nose that had been hit once too often, and an active toothpick being worked at the side of his mouth. The blue ink of a tattoo peaked above the collar of his dirty T-shirt. His day job was with a local body shop. I was less interested in that than I was with what he liked to do at night.

He looked at me suspiciously as we sat down. Guys like G.G. don't generally like cops, but he was smart enough not to show it...at least not too much.

"What can I do for you Detective Ansini?" He said it like a wise guy in a Martin Scorsese movie. I get a charge from guys like this. He's in a world of trouble, in jail, nobody cares enough to bail him out, and he's trying to act like a big shot.

"You can tell me where you got the drugs." I was not in the mood to play games or pretend that I wanted to make friends.

"What drugs?" Martin Scorsese act two, scene

one.

"Cut the shit, G.G. Tell me where you got the drugs and maybe I can help you sleep in your own bed one of these days." I could see the wheels turning. G.G. may not have been in the running to become a Jeopardy contestant but he seemed to sense what people in his situation might call "an opportunity." He waited a second or two.

"Sorry Detective Ansini," he said. "I've had a bad couple of days." He rubbed a big bruise on his cheek. No "zigged when he should have zagged" quips. I already gave him higher marks than Furman Junior or Maybe a D+. And, he was a lot easier to take than old man Furman.

I explained to him that I wasn't in the mood to play games and that the pot and the Fentanyl were a big problem for him. Especially the opiate, known on the street as Apache or China Girl or Tango or a number of other things. It seemed an unbroken flow from China, Canada and Mexico, not to mention from illegal U.S. labs, making its way to all corners of the nation. I gave him a big pitch on the department's current priority, driven by demands from the politicians and the public to get that stuff off the streets.

"Any idea how many people die from opioids"

He shook his head.

"Fifteen hundred this year alone right here. Almost double two years ago."

No reaction.

"The number of townies is about the same as killed in Viet Nam."

A quizzical expression.

"Do you know about Viet Nam?"

"Some war?"

Hard to believe he was that stupid.

"You do heroin."

"No."

"Because a lot of people mix Fentanyl with heroin."

No reaction.

"It's a killer combo."

"Apache's cheaper."

"Unless it kills you."

He shrugged his shoulders.

I told him that's what's called a major league epidemic. He responded with what he apparently thought was his tough guy look.

I told him it was all a formula for hard time for him. I let that sink in. And I hinted that maybe we could help him in return.

Guys playing tough guys normally go one way in these situations. They want to shout from the mountaintop that they don't snitch...they want to be quiet as clams and tell the world that "I ain't talking and you can't make me."

Nine times out of ten we can make them open up by giving them a "we can lock 'em up" look, and a "throw away the key" talk then segue into something a little less onerous, like "you think your girlfriend's going to stay home knitting while you're away?" There are variations on that. Most of the scenarios work most of the time. But not all of the time. For most of the conversation he gave me the thousand yard stare, unseeing and unfocused.

We went around like this a bit more on all of this before he brought his attention back to our limited space. And when he did he gave me a nice surprise. Seems Mark Furman Junior was pretty active in the opioid market.

G.G. and Junior had a bit of a history. Turns out they got to know each other when Goodstrich was a mower of lawns for the Furman enterprise before he moved up the minimum wage employment ladder to the body shop. They stayed in touch. Literally and figuratively as it turns out. G.G. provided the pot. Mark the opioids.

Some of the guys in the bar fight were regular customers and had a beef with the way prices were increasing. They were not into supply and demand arguments.

G.G. and I had a shorter conversation about where Furman got his stash. He told me he had no idea. He was convincing when he asked me if I believed a guy like Furman trusts a guy like him? I told him I'd do what I could to get him some help in his current predicament. He seemed grateful. I was the grateful one. Fact is I could be of limited help. I would try, but he was in some petty deep shit and if things moved along he might have to help himself...in court.

While I would have loved to make the bust, we do have our little pieces of turf in the cop shop. So, I took what I had to the narcotics guys. They could take it from there. I'd thought I might get a little glory out of it all, but all I got was the potential satisfaction of seeing a fairly good sized opioid operation plowed under.

It played out in less than a week. The arrest, the beating, my visit, some ratting by a barroom friend and no doubt some editorial comment from the old man...apparently put young Mark into deep panic mode. He was under surveillance. Our guys were interested in training dogs to scope out opioids, especially Fentanyl. They had borrowed a German Shepard that had been highly trained in Canada for a department on the other side of the state.

This was tricky business. Dogs are great at detecting narcotics, but are as sensitive to opioids as humans. They can overdose with too much exposure. If dogs get a good whiff of opioids it can do them serious damage, even kill them. There are many cases on record, including one in Florida where three K-9s overdosed during a federal raid on a home. Law enforcement in the U.S. and Canada are working to train the dogs to react when they detect drugs, but not to sniff them up close.

It was a narcotics officer working with a uniformed cop surveilling him who pulled Mark Furman and his BMW over. It was easy. They waited for him to change lanes illegally. That was all they needed. He gave them a little heat because he was nervous. Never a good idea. They asked him to step out of the car and pet the doggie. The pup did, as it was trained to do, and just sat down and stared at Mark. While the uniformed officer wrote out a ticket for the traffic violation, the other officer walked the dog around the car. The dog sat down by the trunk of the car.

The cop writing the ticket was just finishing when the officer handling the dog asked Mark if he had any objection to his taking a look inside the car. Clearly nervous, Mark said he did. The officer explained that he had probable cause to suspect there were drugs in the car. His options were that Mark could let him look, wait for a warrant, or take the whole issue downtown.

I was told that Mark's legs got rubbery and that the sweat was wetting through his shirt and suit-coat. The officer said that by allowing the search things would go better for him if drugs were found. Mark blubbered something about wanting a lawyer. He was told there'd be plenty of time for that if there were a problem and he was taken into custody.

There was. About a hundred small bottles containing Fentanyl capsules in various amounts. The uniformed officer made a call on his radio. Some other cars were quickly on the scene. Mark was informed of his arrest, was Mirandized and taken downtown for questioning.

The next day, officers showed up at the Furman offices and the Furman household with warrants where more Fentanyl was found. About fifty thousand dollars in cash was found in a lock box in Mark Junior's room. That would not work to the advantage of other members of the Furman family.

They were also brought in beginning an investigation that was likely to last for a while. And, it no doubt gave them time to consider whether it was a really a good idea to have reestablished the living arrangement for their nuclear family when Mark got out of college.

Media coverage was extensive and more than a little sensational given the prominence of the family involved. Still a lot of loose ends, but I thought I'd have to tell McGee that an immigration issue was probably the least of the worries for the Mark Furmans, Senior or Junior.

I had to admit I was very well satisfied with how it was turning out. I still had a fresh image of young Mark trying to dig the wax out of his ear. He was digging out of something much deeper now. And, the old man. He was going to be getting fewer invitations to the clubs and dinners. Too bad. He was off the A-list at least temporarily while the wheels of justice spun on.

The lieutenant who ran the Drug Enforcement Unit was tickled. We had a few good laughs over it all. He was grateful that I had kick-started the investigation. He had a good bust, and good publicity for the unit. There was probably more to come.

But to him the best news was the dog. The real hero, he told me, was not me for putting Furman on their radar, though it was "much appreciated." It was the dog. He was certain he could convince the "boys upstairs" that they should invest in one specially trained in opioid detection. He was salivating over the thought that the cash seized in Mark's bedroom would be more than enough to buy one and to train it. Maybe two.

MCGEE

"Think you're ready to die Jeff?" Not a fun way to open a conversation at Nellie's. But Jeff and I have talked about a lot of things over the course of our relationship there. This was not one of them. I don't know why I brought it up, but death had been on my mind. Fred and Mary. References to Jennifer. My current health issues. Hell, when you reach the eight decade mark, it's something that crosses your mind. Mortality!

During the early part of our lives, it's all about immortality and being invulnerable. That's what makes great fighter pilots. It's not about beating the odds. It's about not knowing there are odds...risks. What twenty year old thinks about dying? It's all about living.

When do we recognize the inevitability of death? For me it's nothing new. Every ache, every pain, every skipped step, every sleepless night, every visit to the doctor has me asking the question. How much time is left? Is this it? Today? Tomorrow? Next month? Next year?

I tried to think of it as if life were a light just going out. Now light. Then dark. Someone once told me that death was like life in the womb. No consciousness. No awareness. No light. I could buy all of that as long as the light didn't go out for me in a hospital bed with tubes in my arms and vertical stitches on my chest. I have end- of-life directives.

I believed in what John Gunther said; "live while you live, then die and be done with it." I did not buy into the heaven-hell-eternal joy-flying angel myths. No "marching in formation toward the sunset" for me. No tunnels with bright lights and loved ones waiting and waving like aircraft carrier deckhands bringing in screaming jets.

They say that the real pain of death is felt by surviving loved ones. I had no one to mourn.

Jeff heard my question, but did not respond right away. He was looking at something as if he were searching for a friend getting off the last car of a long train.

"You know something I don't?" he finally said, after taking a long swallow.

"No. It's just something I've been thinking about lately. Thinking about it a lot."

"Me too. A little more lately. Seems I've got a problem."

It was a head snapping comment. I was taken

aback and must have looked it.

"I had some tests a week or so ago. I'd not been feeling so hot. So, of course, they brought me in for tests." He made a sound meant to be a sign of distaste. "They don't miss any opportunities any more to order tests. They must cost a fortune. Thank god for Medicare."

He took a deep breath. "Long story short, they found a couple of shadows or spots on my liver. I'm going back for more tests in a day or two." He clasped his hands, fingers interlocked like a prisoner awaiting a verdict.

I wanted him to talk although I didn't like what I was hearing. Catharsis, I thought, remembering Travis McGee in one of his books saying, "Illness is an ego trip." When we're ill, especially seriously ill, it's difficult to think of anyone but yourself.

"I don't like the sound of it," he said. "But the old body breaks down sooner or later." Another swallow of beer. "I've concluded that life is like a train ride. The engine starts out slowly...chug, chug, chug...and then it begins to pick up speed. When it gets to our age, it's a bullet train racing toward the end station. Every day, every week, every month goes faster." He rubbed his chest. "I'm on the bullet train right now."

I was stunned. Almost speechless and in retrospect almost wish I had been. "Jeff, I don't know what to say. You look great." I instantly regretted saying that. "I'm really sorry to hear you're going through something like this." I reached over and put my hand on his. "If there's anything I can do…" I regretted saying that too.

He shook his head slowly from side to side and raised a finger to stop me. I'm glad he did. Words are difficult to come by in a situation like this. The right words. Most people grope reflexively with nonsense like…"You'll be okay." "They can do miracles these days." "I'll have you in my prayers." And like, "Anything I can do?" as if there were anything anyone can do when uncertainty and anguish are cohorts.

"Too much beer," he said, trying to lighten things up.

"Or not enough," I replied going for the assist.

If it's cancer, I thought, there won't be much to smile about. Liver cancer. It was the third time liver cancer had intruded on my world. My wife Holly was brought down quickly. My aunt was diagnosed with it on Valentine's Day of all days, and was dead by the Fourth of July. That was a long time ago. Medical science had made a lot of progress over the decades since. Not enough to help Holly. Instead of six months it might prolong things twenty or thirty months. Maybe more. But the outcome was usually the same. It was a tough bullet to dodge and two people close to me had been unable to get out of its way.

Why the hell, I thought, did I have to bring up

the subject of death during a sunny afternoon with a good friend in a neighborhood bar? He didn't need to know what I knew about liver cancer.

We sat in silence and I thought about all the friends and family I had outlived. That's the worst part of being lucky enough to age. Parents go, siblings go, spouses go, close friends go, and one day you realize you're about the last man standing. The title of the film, *The Loneliness of the Long Distance Runner* popped into my head. Loneliness was more than a title. It was a way of life for people like me. Life without Jeff, my last real friend, if it came to that, would leave a big hole in my life. I remembered a John D. MacDonald-Travis McGee's three eternal words... "Please not yet...please not yet."

I'd been lucky myself. My health was not great, but apparently the major parts of this old machine still worked okay. Aches and pains and such, but I was not facing what my friend Jeff had in front of him. I was hopeful modern medicine would come to the rescue, and I would pray for him. I just wouldn't say it out loud.

"I'll be having some new tests later in the week," he repeated. He spoke softly and sounded as if he were resigned to potential bad news. "Fact is Trav, if it is the Big C and it's terminal, I won't want to wind up in a hospital with tubes and all that. I've got a DNR...Do Not Resuscitate directive. I want them to pull the plug."

I nodded. "Me too."

"It's really time to change the subject," he said. "I don't want to begin feeling sorry for myself. And...I don't want to drag you into my problems." That was so Jeff. He was that kind of guy. A gentle, considerate soul.

"Well, have you been reading about the Furmans in the paper?"

His eyes brightened and he looked more relaxed.

"Yeah. You know it took me a while before I realized that they were the ones you were talking about when you were becoming a customs and immigration agent." He smiled.

I did too although I was still embarrassed about having concocted my scenario. "Well, they may not have been running illegals, but they sure seem to have had something going with those drugs."

"Careful Trav. Remember, they haven't been convicted of anything yet. Aren't you...old reporter friend...supposed to throw in an "allegedly" from time to time?"

"Let's go with 'former' reporter. I can say what I want now. A trunkful, then a houseful, of Fentanyl is pretty hard to explain."

We went over some of the other details. I told Jeff that I had gotten a call from Detective Ansini. He was pretty proud of himself for having alerted Drug Enforcement and had called to thank me for putting that bug in his ear. He had told me that the kid was a real baby, and that the old man was a jerk.

"Ansini got a kick of hearing that young Furman almost wet his pants during the traffic stop. I remember when I met him he was trying to play the big man in the board room when talking about how much it would cost me to join the company 'family.' And the old man confronted Ansini after he visited the kid." I was encouraged to see Jeff's grin.

"Apparently the dad thinks he can skate. Connections and all. Ansini says the case is pretty tight and that the mayor and the cops are tired of the opioid epidemic and want to make an example. It's all moving pretty fast. We'll see."

We were sitting close to the door at Nellie's. It opened causing a momentary stream of blinding sunlight to sweep across our table. Because of the backlight I couldn't see who was entering. But once the door closed, it was a surprise to see Troy and Jenny Hacker standing just inside. She was giving the room a critical onceover as if to make sure it was up to her standards. Troy had no doubt and moved toward an empty table

I watched them with interest. Of all couples, this one was not the pair I would have guessed knew about, much less deigned to frequent, my favorite tavern.

Nellie's was not Club 54, but it was not at all unpleasant, unless you were uncomfortable in a quiet place, nice ambiance, good sandwiches and a good selection of imported beer. Shiny oak panel-ing and exposed brick gave it a colonial touch.

Jenny was dressed for the next real estate deal. Tailored pantsuit, freshly frosted hair and lots of bling that jingled with every haughty stride. I could see Nellie appraising her from behind the long, glistening, oak bar. Andy was impassive as usual. I wondered what he might have been think-ing. Jenny passed him with an expression that read *are you kidding me? I've got to get out of here.*

As they reached the table, Jenny seemed to have made up her mind with a look I interpreted as one of disapproval. Knowing her, I was certain she didn't want to sign on or sign in. She was slum-ming. Maybe if she had a Corolla in her garage...

Nonetheless she plopped down when Troy pulled out her chair. I saw her whisper something to him. I would bet it was something like, "Let's get out of this dump."

Nellie, about fifty, was a little overweight, with stringy hair that once had been dark now graying. She was not one for putting on airs. She knew who her clientele was. She was wearing her customary jeans, and one of her vast array of T-shirts. This one featured International Harvester although her generous breasts made it hard to read. She saved her favorite, Che Guevara, for special occasions like Cinco de Mayo. I don't think she knew Che was not Mexican or perhaps she didn't care.

At this moment, she also wore a sardonic smile

as she watched her new customers. I was sure she was thinking what I was thinking. She waited a moment before moving to the Hacker table, probably to determine whether Jenny would find an escape route.

When it was clear she wouldn't, Nellie approached, offered menus, took drink orders, and left to retrieve them. Jenny studied the menu with obvious disfavor taking a lot longer than needed to consider the limited fare. She is a piece of work, I thought, while Troy glanced at the menu and put it down. He drummed his fingers impatiently waiting for her to decide.

I looked at Jeff and rolled my eyes. He had picked up on the newcomers. Not surprising because we knew most of the regulars and very few of them ever came in looking like Mrs. Hacker.

I gave him the old jailhouse whisper telling him very briefly who they were and how I had come to know them. As I did so, I also wondered if I should go over and say hello. They could live without it, but I was curious about them. While Jenny was still deciding, I decided I would.

"How's the garden?" I asked as I approached the table. Troy looked up, surprised. Jenny did too, and managed a bit of a smile of recognition. I sensed she was trying to remember my name. Troy had a warm hello. Jenny managed a nod that measured about 28 degrees Fahrenheit.

"Welcome to my world," I said, gesturing with

both arms outstretched. "Nice to see you guys."

Troy looked a little confused. "You own this place?"

I detected some movement from Jenny with the words "own this place." The realtor's antennae were on full alert.

"No, I just come here often enough to have sent both of Nellie's kids through college." No reaction. "I'm a regular."

"The garden's great," said Troy backtracking on the conversation.

"Better than the gardener, I'll bet."

Troy's confusion was apparent. Jenny looked at me like I was crazy.

"Oh, it's just that the parent company of the folks who put it in for you are in a bit of hot water. Seems they may be in the drug business. Allegedly." That was my homage to Jeff.

"What?" Troy was clearly in the dark on the story.

"National American Landscaping, it's local, owns the company that did the work on your "Back 40." Troy liked the reference. "It's a franchise deal."

"For god's sake Troy, don't you read the paper?" Jenny now being heard from in sharped, clipped tones. She grudgingly gave him a synopsis of the story with enough detail to show that she did read the papers. He shook his head as if it was all news to him, which it obviously was.

"Thanks again for letting me look around the

other day," I said. "It was a big help."

I turned to Jenny hoping I neither looked nor sounded too disingenuous. "How's the pup?"

"Fine." She had a way with words, or should I say "word."

"Mary Haller tells me you may be selling her house...that maybe you're going into business for yourself."

A funny sound from Troy. Either a stifled cough, or something that sounded like whew.

That breathed new life into Jenny. She reached into a purse the size of a backpack and retrieved a card. It read *Hacker Homes. Time to sell? I'll sell it. And if I don't I'll buy it.* Two phone numbers were prominent.

"That's a different approach." I remembered Mary telling me of that business plan.

"Yeah. There's a gal in Missouri racking up some big bucks. She says she will sell the house or buy it herself. I'm giving it a try." She smiled. The temperature finally above the freezing level. Apparently her thermostat only worked when things were about her or on her terms.

"Troy," she added, "Isn't so sure." She gestured toward him dismissively.

He flushed as his finger tapping picked up in intensity, let's say from three to ten, each beat transmitting a duel message. First one...bitch! Second one...is this small talk ever going to end? If you didn't get the full message that way, his pissed off expression finished the job.

"Good luck. I'll hang on to this and spread the word."

I put Jenny's card in my breast pocket. "Any luck with Mary's place?"

"She's on the fence. You know, the husband and all."

"Yeah, I know. What she really needs is closure. A death certificate so she can collect some insurance and move on."

I thought to myself if she knew Mary was aware of what the Hackers thought about Fred's bolting...or being buried in the basement...she'd never get a whiff of that sale.

"She told me." She produced a big, phony smile. "A nice price on the house would help. Thanks for 'spreading the word.' And if you can, put in a good word with Mary. I'd like to help her." A big smile. "How about you? Ready to sell?"

"No, but when I am I'll give you a call. Nice seeing you guys."

I turned to return to Jeff. Miss Sunshine was not through. "What do you recommend? I was hoping for soup and a salad, but it's not on the menu."

"You can't miss with the pastrami," I said. "On dark rye. And, the slaw's terrific."

She didn't look as if that would likely fit the bill. She gave a little wave goodbye as if she were drying her nails as Nellie approached with their drinks. A Dos Equis for him. A Mimosa for her.

Nellie gave me a sly eye roll as she placed their drinks on the table. It told me this is the first Mimosa anyone's ever ordered in this place. She was also asking how I might know these creatures. I hoped for Nellie's sake the Mimosa met Jenny's standard. Or there'd be hell to pay.

I got back to our table and watched the happy couple exchanging words. I could not hear them, but the discussion appeared to be, let's call it, "spirited."

I gave Jeff an abridged version of the conversation, including my observation that the Hackers wouldn't be a couple very long. They just didn't seem like a very good match. Jeff didn't care. He had his own problems. We continued our conversation for a few minutes and left. I noticed Jenny went for a grilled cheese...Troy for the pastrami.

There are times I feel my world is shrinking, at least in terms of my cast of characters. I didn't have a whole lot of friends. Acquaintances, yes. Friends, no. I didn't have much patience for small talk and for contriving reasons to "get together." Jeff was my buddy. We could move in and out of each other's orbit as frequently or infrequently as we chose. No pressure. We always found something to talk about. And, if there was nothing to say we were comfortable not saying anything.

I worried about him and wondered how the

new tests he'd mentioned had gone. I called and he told me that the doctors wanted to do some exploratory surgery. He was apprehensive, but wanted to get it over with sooner rather than later. He gave me the particulars and I promised to visit. He declined my offer to buy him a beer at Nellie's.

Detective Ansini had told me that the Furman case was on the fast track. The morning paper confirmed it. There was a brief story indicating that a preliminary hearing was scheduled for that day. It got a little space, presumably because of family prominence, and the opioid connection. The paper was on an anti-opioid crusade, so this otherwise obscure court matter made page three.

The story told readers that Mark Furman, Junior, had pleaded not guilty at an earlier arraignment, was out on bond, and that no charges had been filed against Furman Senior or other family members, although a large amount of Fentanyl had been found at the Furman home and at the corporate office. "There was no evidence at the moment," the paper reported, "that anyone else was involved." The "at the moment" line got me thinking that Furman Senior might still be in a jam, or that the paper's editors were hopeful he would be. If so, his connections with people in high places would provide copy for a good long while.

We also learned that a well known local criminal defense attorney by the name of Dowd was on the job for Furman Junior and unsurprisingly assured reporters he was convinced of his client's innocence. I decided to visit the courthouse to get a read on Mr. Dowd, his client, and the case against Mark Furman. I was going to become one of those old people who hang around the courthouse trying to fill their lives with courtroom reality rather than looking for the fictionalized version on television, where, in all honesty, it was usually much more entertaining.

The courthouse is old, a Gibraltar of granite outside; a forest of wood, I have always considered burled walnut, layering the inside. There are ten courtrooms, two to a floor, and a handy information desk near the security apparatus. It's almost always abandoned, so visitors are on their own.

No real trouble getting in. A lot of trouble getting out if your defense attorney has a bad day. Like most old things it has the smell of old in a comforting sort of way. I asked around and finally found the courtroom in question. Courtroom number 6.

I was early and joined a few old guys who were waiting for the show...any show...to help fill their day. I sat in an empty row and watched some of the other oldsters chat it up. I guessed they were regulars and started conversations with each other as they wandered from courtroom to courtroom. This courtroom was like all the familiar counterparts, right out of Perry Mason and the world of Atticus Finch.

Eventually, the room began to fill. A few more old guys. A couple of reporters arrived and took seats, flipping notebooks, ready for action. Mark Furman and counselor Dowd showed up and huddled at the desk designated for the defense. And, Detective Paul Ansini, apparently taking a little time off the crime fighting trail to savor the fruits of his work sidled in. We nodded and smiled. He took a seat near the door.

Preliminary hearings can be interesting. And, for defendants, crucial. In sense, it's a trial without being a trial. It's basically what determines if there will be a trial. The prosecution makes its case with a recitation of what evidence it has, and whether it merits a full blown proceeding. The defense tries to punch holes in it reaching for dismissal. Then the judge decides whether there's enough evidence to kick the case up to the next level. From what I knew about it all, it was going to be an exercise in futility for Mr. Dowd.

The judge entered. We all stood. He rapped the gavel and the proceeding began. The prosecutor was a stunning black woman with a spellbindingly mellifluous voice, part Barbara Jordan part Nina Simone. Which one she used seemed to depend on which one she needed from one moment to the next to be most effective.

She was an imposing figure. Six feet tall, with

skin as black as coal that almost glistened as she spoke. Her name was DeNeisha Trotter. Bad guys called her DeNasty because she was when she had to be. And, the badder they were the more she earned the nickname.

The media loved her. She'd been elected in a big upset, sending a 20 year veteran prosecutor back to private practice. Then she'd been reelected by a huge margin. She knew her stuff, and she was ambitious. That's why she was handling this case personally. A conviction might anger some of the Furman family friends, but would solidify her support among those most vulnerable to an unfair justice system whom she championed.

She made her case very efficiently going over the traffic stop and all that transpired there. Two officers testified. One went over the skills and training of the dog. The other testified as to the amount of Fentanyl found in the car.

Dowd tried to make a case that the stop was illegal but got nowhere.

A character by the name of Gary Goodstrich took the stand for Trotter. He was awaiting trial on charges of possession of drugs and illegal possession of a firearm. He was entertaining. He "respectfully" asked that he be addressed as G.G. He got an immediate taste of DeNasty. "Is your given name Gary? She asked.

"Yes."

"Well if it's good enough for your parents, it's

good enough for this court."

"Yes ma'am. Thank you ma'am." He was not up for a fight.

Gary went on to tell the world how he bought Fentanyl from Furman, not only for himself but enough to make a few extra bucks selling to his buddies. Seems G.G. and Mark Junior got acquainted when G.G. was doing landscaping work for one of the company's local franchises. They met quite by chance on one of the jobs and struck up a conversation. Gary made a crack about landscaping and grass and Mark got the joke. They continued the conversation over a beer at a local dive and a collaboration was born.

Dowd did his best to discredit. G.G. He had plenty to work with, but Goodstrich had pointed his finger straight at Furman and there was no turning away from that.

Trotter blew Dowd out of the water on his attempts to get in something positive on Mark's character and lack of a criminal record. She allowed as how given the evidence, Mr. Dowd really didn't have very much to work with on that score.

The judge agreed and set a trial date at the end of the month. As Ansini had indicated, this was on a fast track. Furman and Dowd left the courtroom. Dowd looked as proud as if he'd won a dismissal of charges. He'd try the case and lose it and still get his fee.

Furman's slumped shoulders told his story. Although the outcome could not have come as a surprise to him, he hunched forward like someone going to the guillotine. For him, it was the beginning of not the best of times, but rather, the worst of times.

The courtroom cleared quickly. Detective Ansini and I were among the last to leave. I had the feeling he wanted me to catch up. He waited at the heavy door and held it open for me as I approached. I thanked him. He lifted his chin.

"What do you think?"

I pointed toward the door as it thumped shut. "Like the door...open and shut. He doesn't seem to have much going for him."

"I think he'll change his plea to guilty and hope for a deal from the judge." Ansini spoke as someone who had seen this play before. He probably had.

"He really thought he could outsmart everybody." Ansini buttoned his coat. "The story I get is that he hated the family business and really wanted no part of it. He was trying to bankroll his escape." He paused. "Dad was apparently a prick to him."

"Why did he live at home then?"

"To save money I guess."

"Do you think the old man was in on it? Lots of Fentanyl on his property."

"Don't know. I'll bet our favorite prosecutor would like his scalp. But she would be very, very careful. He's got contacts she may need one day. If he's ever indicted he'll come in with a legal team that'll make Dowd seem like a rookie Public Defender."

We walked a few steps when he asked, "What did you think of the star witness?"

"Goodstrich? Seemed like a real loser."

"He's between a rock and a hard place in more ways than one. He and Furman had more than a business relationship." He let that sink in. "They liked to rub noses, if you know what I mean. Turns out that bar fight was less about supply and demand and more about who hooked up that night." He shook his head as if trying to understand that dynamic. "I think he and his boyfriend would not like prison if that's the way it turns out. He's banking on his testimony getting him a better deal."

He stopped and I did too. "I wonder how Furman likes it under the bus? Don't believe it when they say there's honor among thieves. Guys like G.G. excuse me Gary...very predictable." He chuckled..."how did you like that move? Guys like him would sell their mother."

"Trotter didn't mess with him."

On cue, the prosecutor came toward us as we stood outside on the sidewalk in front of the courthouse. She was walking quickly, obviously in a hurry. She stopped when she saw us...or rather him.

"Hello Paul," she said, smiling broadly revealing an astonishing display of the whitest teeth I had ever seen, whiter still in contrast with her deep black skin.

"How's my favorite prosecutor?" He asked. "Nice job in there." She Liked that and gave a slight, modest bow.

Ansini introduced me and I told her how impressed I was with her "performance" in court.

Another slight bow. "Oh, that wasn't a performance," she joshed. "That was a pleasure. Two lowlifes. One a dirt bag, the other a dirt bag in a clean shirt with a big job and a big house and a big daddy." She turned to Ansini. "Pauli my man, you've got to bring me more of these boys so we can put them away." A little giggle. "I gotta run." And, she was off.

"I'll do my best," he said. But she was already out of earshot. A woman on the fast track I thought, and wherever she wanted to go today, tomorrow or whenever, she'd get there in fine style.

Ansini watched her turn the corner. "She's something else. No nonsense." He reflected for a moment. "She's going places. She's got an agenda and she has a constituency. I'll bet she's attorney general before I retire." He smiled and I couldn't tell if he was hoping she would, or would not.

He held out his hand to shake mine. "Let me buy you a beer one of these days. You got this whole thing started. I appreciate it."

"I've got nothing but time," I said as we shook

firmly. "I'm thirsty now. Nellie's is right down the street."

He shook his head. "Another time. I've got places to go and people to meet." He smiled, "gotta keep the city safe you know."

"Any time then," I said as he turned to cross with the light. "Give me a call," I hollered. He waved his arm in the air without turning. I thought...so long until next time Detective Ansini.

JENNY

I really think Mary Haller would be a good place to start. She's vulnerable and alone. She wants to sell and move. Her husband has bolted. She needs the money. Should be an easy mark. And I could arrange for the cash if I have to buy it myself. I don't think I'll have to. What I need to do is get the ball rolling. Hacker Homes is on the move.

The visit with Mary was not as productive as I hoped. She wanted to sell, but the husband thing was a problem. She wanted that resolved before taking the next step. She said something about wanting a neat package...insurance and house sale at the same time. But no death certificate, no insurance. No insurance, no sale.

She was very nice, but a white bread kind of person. The day I went over she had just started putting ads in the paper advertising her attempt to have her husband declared dead. It's a state law or something, and she had to do it for several weeks to see if anyone objected to her attempt. She complained that it was something she should have done months ago, but no one had told her. That would not solve the problem, but it had to be part of the process. The big problem was the death certificate.

I sympathized with her over the loss of her husband and probably made a mistake when I joked that I sometimes wished mine would disappear. She didn't get it and didn't like it and looked at me like I had slapped her face. I think I got out of it okay when I said I didn't mean it the way it sounded, and explained that Troy and I were not eye to eye on some things but had a great marriage. She seemed to buy that. One of my better sales jobs.

So, we met but I didn't come away with a deal. I'll get back to her in a week or so. I was sorry I had told Troy that I was going to pitch Mary. He would certainly ask how it went and would be pissy if I told him I didn't get a contract.

He can be such a dick sometimes. Sometimes? Most of the time. I think the problem is he's jealous. I've been making pretty good money and he's limping along trying to sell insurance. I make more on one good sale than he does on a basketful of policies. And, he took a chunk of that big deal I had with the condo development and put in that ridiculous garden. I'm glad I got the Mercedes before he started all of that. The way he was going there wouldn't have been anything left. "The car will last a few years, the garden will last forever," he said. It may last forever, but we won't be living in this house forever, at least I won't be, and you can't take a stinkin' garden with you.

When I told him that, it shook him up. I think he loves me. But I don't love him that way. In fact, I wonder if I love him at all. I'm young, my whole life is ahead of me. I'm successful and I'm starting my own business. And, I'm good looking. There are plenty of fish...rich ones...swimming in the sea. Troy was treading water.

I tried not to tell him about the meeting with Mary, but he kept asking. I finally told him that it's on hold for the moment...just for the moment. He laughed at me and told me I'd never get the sale. Now I had something to prove. Daisy watched in the corner. She's so cute and gave me a good excuse to get out of the house.

As I walked with the dog, I made a decision. I decided that if Troy thought my inability to close a deal with Mary Haller was so funny, I'd give him something really funny to laugh about. Divorce. I made up my mind as Daisy was doing her business. She left a rather large pile on the Haller lawn. When we continued, I saw a curtain close in the Haller house. I had the feeling someone was watching me...us. Mary? The abandoned one?

Troy and I had a long conversation that night.

It did not go especially well, but it went better than I expected. He was not happy with the way things had been going, saw that I was unhappy and agreed to a split. He suggested living apart for a while to determine just how stormy the nuptial waters were, before making a final decision. This was not all done without a fair amount of heated discussion, but after exhausting all the things we didn't like about our lives with each other. We reached an agreement on a trial separation. The thing that frosted me was that he wanted to stay in this house with his beloved garden.

There it was. The damn garden meant more to him than I did. That's okay too. I'm just glad one of the little brown landscapers didn't rape me. I was separating from the garden and would leave it behind...just as I was sure my separation from him would end in divorce and leaving him behind.

Because Troy is Troy, he wanted to go to a lawyer to determine the legal ins and outs of what lay ahead. I told him a trial separation is just that, a trial as in try it, if it doesn't work, it's Togethersville. If we try it and like it, we move on. Nonetheless, he wanted some legal advice as to whether we needed to sign any kind of legal agreement. "Okay," I said, "Set it up. I'm sleeping in the guest bedroom."

Two days later we were in the lawyer's office going over the definitions of trial separation...legal separation...divorce...division of assets, and all sorts of legal mumbo jumbo. I just wanted to get on with it. Troy and I decided we'd discuss what route we wanted to take over lunch.

I never heard of Nellie's place until Troy suggested we stop there. It looked like a dump to me, but Troy was being assertive and said he and "the boys"...whoever they were...often ate there. The "boys," it turns out, were his office buddies. Those I had met were all losers in my book, the kind that specialize in fart jokes and are obsessed with women's boobs and butts.

I could see that this was a guy's place. Not my vibe. All wood and brick. Dark. Not the kind of dark for privacy but rather the kind of dark to save on the electricity bill. No tablecloths, a long bar, and a billion bottles of different beers behind it. I don't know what was going on in the kitchen, but it smelled like sauerkraut mixed with god knows what. The woman behind the bar looked like a refugee from some farm, dressed to kill in a T-shirt and jeans. All she was missing was a John Deere cap. And the old guy in the corner...he looked dead. And, was that a baseball bat on the chair?

Troy and I had just sat down when the garden guy...what's his name? McGee, I think, came up to the table. He was a nice enough old guy but after all the chit-chat with the lawyer I was not in the mood to make small talk. Because he was so interested in Troy's landscape job, I had this guy figured for a loser too. What I really needed was a Mimosa and to try and figure out what to eat in this joint.

He asked about Daisy and he really seemed interested in my new company. I remembered that he was friends with Mary Haller, so I gave him a pitch and asked if he could help me get to Madam Haller. He indicated he would. Wouldn't that be something if this old guy could help me put that one over the top. I kind of think he'll talk to her. Troy acted like a jerk all the while, drumming his fingers, looking for attention I guess.

When McGee left we got down to business and worked it all out. There wasn't much. Trial separation. I'd find a place. He'd stay at the house and take care of the dog if I could not find a place that accepted pets. No financial problems. I'd pay my own way. He'd pay housing expenses. We'd give it six months and get together periodically to see where we were and where it was all going. I thought I knew and I'm guessing Troy did too.

An hour later we were back at my almost former home. That's where I found Daisy dead in the back yard.

I couldn't believe it. I lost it. I could not control the tears...the shortness of breath. Daisy. Dead! Her body lay on the grass. As I stood over her, she looked like a horse stretching for the finish line. Her tongue was hanging limply from the side of her blue-black lips, visible in areas that were not covered by a sickening frothy white foam. It still looked moist. Flies were attentive. My lovely dog looked ugly. I could not stand it. I wanted to barf.

Troy told me he thought she'd been poisoned. How would he know? Who in the world would do such a thing to an innocent dog? Why? I was beside myself. This was supposed to be a happy day. I could hardly catch my breath from crying.

I wondered if Troy might have done it. He did not love the dog as I did. He could take it or leave it. Mostly leave it. It was my dog he said.

We'd argued over it. I wanted the dog to sleep in our bed. He didn't. We'd compromised. Daisy slept on a mat at the foot of the bed. But somehow she managed to find a way to slink onto the covers in the middle of the night as we both slept. It was a nightly ritual that ended with Troy, cursing, swiped her off the bed. On those occasions when Troy was away on business, Daisy and I cuddled.

Troy and I had a pretty intense argument over putting a doggie door out to the garden. I won that one. I feel guilty now, because that's why Daisy was outside while we were gone. And, that's how someone got poison to her. But who?

I have to admit that Troy was sweet. He could be kind. He said I should go upstairs and rest and that he'd take care of the dog. By that he meant removing it from the garden. He said he'd bury Daisy there if I wanted, or take it someplace to be disposed of. "The garden?" I screamed. "No fucking way."

I ran to the garage and jumped into my car. I drove away as fast as I could. I didn't know where I was going. I just drove, and drove and drove until there were no more tears. When I got back, I could not have told you where I'd been. The dog was gone. Troy was waiting. He told me the folks at the Humane Society were sure the dog had been poisoned. They wanted to do an autopsy to make sure about the poison. Especially if we wanted to report it to the police.

I told him what difference would that make? Anybody could have done it. Someone who hated dogs? Cruel kids? Maybe she ate a dead critter. We'd never find out. The dog was dead. Nothing would bring her back. Troy agreed and said he'd call the Humane Society. They could cremate Daisy if I wanted. I said sure.

Looks like I would be taking Daisy with me after all when I started my new life. But in a box. And I planned to find that new life as quickly as possible, and find a place of my own the next day. I would never return to this home. I could never be there again without seeing the dog dead among the shrubs and ugly statues. Cupid for Christ's sake! What a laugh.

I could not shake the nagging notion that Troy might have given me a dead Daisy as a little going away present. In some ways that made sense. He'd have no dog to care for after I moved out. He knew that was coming before we visited the lawyer. And he'd be giving me the finger at the same time. How cowardly is that? Yup. All the more reason to get out of Dodge.

Now, what am I going to call my new company? Hacker Homes won't work. Neither will the phone number. Shit! And after all the money I spent on those business cards. Maybe "Gotta Deal" or something like that.

TROY

I know she thinks I killed the dog. I did not and I could not, but Jenny has a full head of steam right now. She's on a tear. I'm sorry about Daisy. I didn't love the dog but I didn't hate her either. But, she was Jenny's little girl and Jenny took care of her rain or shine. I doubt we'll ever find out who poisoned her. I guess I might have played a role when I caved on her request for a doggie door out to the back. She said she had a vote, and had the money to do it herself. And that's what she did. What choice did I really have.

I have bigger worries now. I don't think a trial separation and being apart, brings people together.

What has happened to her? She was so much fun when we met. Bright, pretty, energetic. Up for anything. Great assets when she got interested in real estate, and realized that she was good at it. I was all for it. She was happy and the extra money that started to come in was more than helpful. But,

it didn't take long before she became more interested in that...and later the dog...than in me. She
was spending more time on the job and less and
less time with me. And, as she was more and more
successful, she seemed to even resent me more and
more. Within three years she was making twice
as much as I was. It made her more independent,
and the more independent she became, the less she
would need me. It did something else too. She
became bitchy. She did not laugh at me out loud,
but I could feel her laughter when I could not see
it. I could feel the marital waters become increasingly choppy. I should have confronted her. Was I
afraid?

When she closed on that super-sized condo
building and brought home that big commission
check I could tell a corner had been turned and
that it was the beginning of the end for us. She
joked that she was the big earner in the family. She
joked, but there's truth somewhere in every joke. I
felt she wanted to hurt me. Why didn't I say something? Why didn't I do something? There were
times when I wanted to slap her silly. Thank God I
didn't do that. That would have been awful.

When she spent all that money on that red
missile, I complained. I thought that money
should go into a savings account. She wouldn't
hear of it. She earned the money, she said, and she
was going to spend it on what she wanted. And
spend she did, like money was going out of style.

Clothes, jewelry, the hairdresser. And, of course, on the dog.

She said I could spend some of it on the landscaping project I was so interested in. It was like she was giving me an allowance or doling out a few dollars to get me to shut up. But, I took the money.

When Fred Haller started being a pain in the ass about the work on the Back 40, she did not support me. She said Haller was right. It was too loud too early and causing too much dust and dirt. It was not only upsetting the Hallers, it was upsetting her! And Daisy. She hated the Back 40 work and everything that went with it. Including the landscapers. I was shrinking her outdoor domain. Daisy didn't tell me that. Jenny did.

She did not like having the Mexicans around all day. She was afraid one of them...or all of them...might rape her. She didn't like the way they looked at her. She wanted me to do something about them. What was I to do, fire them because she thought they might be thinking about an assault? There was never any evidence of that, except in her mind? She called me weak for not at least talking to them. Can you imagine?

She found an excuse to be away from the house as much as she could when they were here. They didn't seem to mind. I'm sure they sensed that she felt she was too good for them. Fact is, I didn't much care for them either. They spoke Spanish all day. They seemed dirty and surly and drank beer at end of every workday sometimes leaving bottles and cans behind. I should have complained about that, but I didn't.

I wondered if she were having an affair. I'm not even sure she could or would. That would mean sharing herself with someone else. That's not the new, hyper-confident, super selfish Jenny. She would not want to share herself with anyone but herself.

The real estate thing was the only thing that turned her on. When that fellow McGee came to our table at Nellie's, the only thing that got her to stop complaining about the place was his question about her new company. She was happy that he seemed enthusiastic. She lit up like a roman candle. I thought he was just being polite. When he left, she became Jenny again. Bitching about the lawyer, Nellie's, and challenging my ability to make enough to live on when she "flew the coup." How's that for describing a trial separation and the likely end of a marriage? "Flying the coup."

She used to talk about earning potential while nagging me about my job and what she called the "earnings arc." Where the hell did she come up with that one? Could I, she wondered, ever get to the point where our incomes were equal? She never missed a chance to point out that selling houses was a lot more lucrative than selling "two-bit" insurance policies. She mockingly wondered why I didn't start *my* own company.

Then when she got the idea to start *hers*, I tried to tell her that her "earnings arc" would likely go south until she could get her feet on the ground. She laughed at me. She wondered what made me think I knew what I was talking about. "You'll see," she said laughing, "You'll see."

Day after day of that sort of thing grinds you down. It's like some kind of Chinese water torture test. Drip, drip, drip.

I guess I'm just weak. No wonder she wants out.

The more I think about it, I'll be happy, even relieved, when she's gone. She's not been a companion, a friend or a wife for months. She's been a judge. And a jury.

But I didn't kill the dog. And I'm glad I didn't kill Jenny.

MARK FURMAN
JR

Holy shit, holy shit, holy shit! I'm in deep shit. That fucking G.G. That fucking police dog. Holy shit, holy shit, holy shit! There's only one way I'm going to get a break on this. Dowd isn't optimistic and is already talking about appeals. So, I'll have to give them something that can get me a better deal. It's going to be painful. But, to thine own self be true, no matter who gets hurt in the process. This will be tough. I'll contact Dowd and tell him I want to talk to the feds. I can give them a big one. It will indeed be painful. But hard time is painful!

G.G. A.K.A. GARY GOODSTRICH

I'll beat this!

ANSINI

I don't want to say that I was caught off guard by being invited to the meeting, but I was very happy to be a part of it. The call came from our guys in Drug Enforcement. The feds wanted a meeting involving the lieutenant and he included me because the scope of their investigation would likely spill over into my bailiwick. The lieutenant was playing it close to the vest when he came by.

"I don't want to get into it now," he said. "The feds have some information they want to discuss. I don't know exactly what's up, but it must have some juice for them to contact us. That's not their favorite thing."

I was intrigued because he was right. The feds usually liked to work on their own. They felt that local cops weren't quite up to their professional standard and that too many fingers in the pie kicked up, not only the possibility, but the probability of a leak. They resented that. And, if there was any credit to be gained at the end of the day, they didn't like to share it. We resented that. Mutual resentment is not the best basis for any collaboration.

The meeting was called for the next day at the local office of the Drug Enforcement Agency. The DEA had a nice suite in the new federal office building downtown which also housed the federal courts, an FBI regional office and various agency field offices. I'd been in the building a few times, always envious of how the feds always seemed to have plenty of money to spend and how they spent it. Boilerplate and concrete block was not in Uncle Sam's lexicon when it came to establishing a presence. It was tinted glass and marble and stainless steel all the way. I guarantee the elevators always worked.

There were five of us. Lieutenant Donn Riggins was our guy. He's a fifty year old veteran with a great record. I respected him a lot. Any black officer with rank had to overcome a lot of hurdles to achieve rank and maintain it. I suspected he might have wondered from time to time why he was swimming in place or treading water rather than splashing in the deep end. If so, it never showed. Maybe at home, but not on the job.

He was a tough cop who grew up where drugs caused a lot of his buddies to die, or wind up in prison. He survived that environment and, as he put it, "went over to the other side" when he joined the department. That wasn't a decision that sat well with some of those old time buddies who'd survived. Suspicion of police was a way of life where he grew up.

Riggins and I sat on the opposite side of our hosts at a large conference table. The two DEA agents were out of the textbook. They were young freshly scrubbed white men with dark suits, white shirts, neutral-colored ties. They were costumed not to attract attention until they were slamming cuffs on a perp's wrist. They identified themselves as Agent Berkowitz and Agent Dougherty. No first names were apparently necessary, as if the relationship was already on a need to know basis.

Another man sat silently in a corner of the room.

After shaking hands, it was Berkowitz who started the conversation.

"Our colleague Agent Bob Lovelear from the FBI is with us." He nodded toward the statue in the corner who said nothing.

"Agent Lovelear is here as an observer, not as a participant." He nodded in the direction of the corner again. I wondered if federal agents had some secret form of non-verbal communication.

Berkowitz got right down to business. "We had an interesting conversation with an attorney by the name of Dowd."

Riggins and I exchanged glances at the name of Dowd.

"He has a client who wants to give us some dope...forgive me...some information on an opioid operation. We called you in as a matter of professional courtesy, and we wanted to talk to you guys to get a little ahead of things before we make any kind of a deal."

"Deal?" I asked.

This time it was Dougherty. "His client's looking at some hard time for distribution of Fentanyl. A pretty fair amount. He wants to ease the pain...there I go again...and thinks we can put in a good word. Maybe get a reduced sentence. Seems his client is wetting his pants."

Riggins laughed. "He's been known to do that. You're talking about Mark Furman, right?"

The two agents nodded.

Riggins looked at me. "We recognized the lawyer's name. Watched him in action...if you can call it that...in court the other day." He scratched an ear. "He doesn't have much to go with." He looked at me for corroboration, then at the two agents. "Not surprised he's looking for some wiggle room. What do you need from us?"

Berkowitz turned to Dougherty with an Alphonse and Gaston expression then took over. "Just tell us what you know, and what your thoughts are about any opioid operation in the neighborhood. The more we know going into this thing, the less they have to deal with. We want to hear what Furman has to say, but the more we know going in, the less we need to give away in any negotiation. We're not interested in dealing with Dowd if we don't have to."

"We like putting bad guys away." Dougherty wanted to get into the act.

"We can do that," said Riggins with a smile. "Why don't we begin with you telling us what you've got?" His smile widened. The Cheshire Cat.

The two agents shuffled in their chairs. Lovelear was bouncing his foot. I didn't think they liked the game when everybody wasn't playing by their rules. Neither spoke for what seemed like a long time. Dougherty ended the silence.

"We don't have it all yet. All we can really say without learning more by talking directly to Furman is that he says that he can point the finger at a good sized opioid operation centered right here. And that he can give us the guy in charge. When we nail everything down and move in, we will probably need you guys, depending on what the structure is. This is a small office. Everybody's busy, so we're proposing we set up a mini-task force ready to move in whatever direction we have to. We're looking at potential federal indictments here, so we'll be taking the lead."

"No surprise there." Riggins chortled as he looked at me. Is that it?"

"Your turn," said Berkowitz.

Riggins and I did our own Alphonse and Gaston routine before he nodded at me to begin.

More comfortable now that the game was afoot pretty much on their terms, the two agents settled in.

I gave them my story beginning with suspicions mentioned to me by a well meaning citizen named McGee who put National American Landscaping on my radar. The trigger was the newspaper story about Mark Furman. I could only say that I was in hunch mode, putting two and two together. I'm not all about coincidences. My antennae were up about him and the incident that got him and the others arrested. I went on about my visit with him and the talk about drugs. But I had nothing to go on. Just a gut feeling that there was more to all of it. I kept it short.

Riggins picked it up from there and gave them the entire story from his unit's perspective. He outlined the arrest, the amount of drugs in the car, and spent more than a little time on the merits of the opioid sniffing dog. It almost seemed as if he were lobbying them. I do know that he was hell bent on getting one of his own one way or another.

Berkowitz and Dougherty listened politely, silently, expressionless, and nodded us on at the appropriate times. I had the feeling we weren't telling them anything of substance that they didn't already know.

It all took about an hour. Riggins ended our part of the conversation with a terse, "That's it." He stared at the two agents. After a few seconds he playfully mocked Berkowitz. "Now, it's your turn."

Berkowitz smiled uneasily. He got it. "Okay. Here's the good part...but it stays with the five of us until I give the green light. Agreed?"

Riggins and I said in unison, "Agreed."

Again, the two agents exchanged glances. Berkowitz gave the floor to Dougherty. "Furman's going to go on the record." He paused. If he was looking for dramatic effect, he achieved it. "He's giving up his father. The opioid operation is run by none other than his father, Mark Furman Senior."

Riggins and I couldn't believe our ears and no doubt showed it. "Uh-huh," said Riggins. "The shit's going to hit the fan."

Dougherty nodded in agreement. "Apparently the kid panicked after his court hearing. His lawyer, Dowd, came by to see us and said the kid would talk. We played it like we weren't all that interested...that he had to sell it."

Berkowitz put a self-satisfied smile front and center. "Apparently we did it right."

"How solid is it?" I asked.

"We'll tell you after we talk with the kid." Berkowitz turned toward Dougherty who unveiled a Grade-A smirk. "We'll bring 'em both in and talk to them separately. Looks like Father's Day is going to be special at the Furman household this year."

He broke into little laugh and was joined by Berkowitz. Tweedledum and Tweedledee with federal benefits...complete with pensions no less.

Riggins and I reacted with head shaking surprise. A brief discussion about fallout followed. Mark Furman Senior had important friends in high places. We all knew that there would be pressure. We would all have roles to play. We all agreed that this case had better be air tight from right now til the very end for all of our sakes. I would rather have been on the outside looking in on this one. Careers could be at risk.

As I returned to the office I remembered Mark Furman Senior intercepting me after my visit with his son. It made more sense to me now that he was such a jerk. He was afraid. Now I know why.

MCGEE

Everyone needs a stuntman. One of the things old people fear the most is falling. I fell. Hard. Broken ankle. Hospital. I wished I had had one of those "I've fallen and I can't get up" things. I didn't but managed to do it with some help from passersby. I tripped over a curb. Went down hard but there were plenty of adult Boy Scout types to help. Cell phones earned a new respect from me as they helped guide in a big white ambulance with pretty flashing lights, whisking me away from my Good Samaritan benefactors.

Is there anything as depressing as a hospital room? Colorless, anti-septic, except for the lurking danger of staph and septic infections, or the flu. Hospitals are a breeding ground for bad things...all of them worse to me than the bad thing I was there for. But there I was. I needed surgery to repair the damage, and was there to stay for at least a couple of days.

I wasn't expecting visitors. So it was quite a surprise when Mary Haller entered my room. I hadn't seen her in a while. She came in smiling. "Well, Trav, it looks like you've gone and done it now."

"Careless. Mary, how did you know I was in the hospital?"

"I ran in to your friend Jeff. He told me. I was in the neighborhood and thought I'd stop by. Did you know he's having surgery in a few days?"

Poor Jeff, I thought. This ankle thing's a pain, but at least I'm not going through what he's going through.

"Jeff's negotiating a very rough patch." I told her what was going on with him. Jeff and I had had a long talk about what he was going through. It was very sad. He was going to make a quick trip to see the grandkids before the surgery. He made it clear he thought it could be the last time he'd ever see them. He was anxious on several fronts. He was more afraid of the surgery than he was about what it might reveal.

She was sympathetic. "Why is it always the good guys?" she asked in almost a whisper.

That began a long conversation. We hadn't talked since I told her about the DNA results. She, of course, was still in limbo about Fred and getting only negative responses from the insurance company. The company still insisted on the legally required documents for proof of death. She was in periodic contact with Detective Ansini. Same old, same old.

She told me that she had put something in the paper that the state required about Fred being missing. It was apparently required in advance of any kind of death declaration, but didn't speed up the process. It was simply a step, and didn't make much sense to me as it was basically just soliciting public comment. Good luck with that.

Her spirits seemed good. She had met with Jenny Hacker about selling the house. She didn't like the woman. A little too pushy. Mary suspected, as I did, that Jenny's business model was quirky, and gave her too much of an incentive to hold back on the sales effort so she could come in on her own with an offer below true value. So, that was on hold. She was thinking about finding another realtor, but felt awkward about that.

Otherwise, life was just a day to day process. Get up. Find ways to fill the hours until it was time to go to bed. Get up the next day and start the routine all over again.

"How are you going to get around?" she asked. "You're going to need crutches for a while."

"Yeah, I guess I'll learn how to hobble about."

"Driving?"

"Not for a while. It's my brake foot." I laughed. "I can't hit the road if I can't stop."

She smiled and suddenly became more animated.

"I have an idea. Why don't you come and stay with me until you can get around a little better? I can feed you, run errands. Or take you on errands...just help you get around in general." The idea seem more and more appealing to her as she spoke.

"What do you think?"

The idea came out of the blue. I hadn't really thought about my incapacity and what it would mean for the next couple of weeks I was certainly going to be housebound for a while but it's not in my nature to ask people for help. I didn't think it would work, but her insistence was persuasive and became more and more appealing. It was an easy solution to a problem I hadn't really considered. So, I agreed, but only on the condition I would pay her. We argued for a bit and settled on a nice dinner out when I could drive. Or even before.

I was released from the hospital the next day. I had insisted on trying out my new crutches, but I was told in no uncertain terms that that wasn't going to happen, that I'd leave in a wheelchair. It was hospital policy, and no doubt a key paragraph in the hospital's litigation prevention plan. Mary escorted me and the nurse as I was wheeled to Mary's car.

Her home was as I remembered it. Cozy. Dated. Books. TV. Stress free. And easy to navigate on what I was now calling "my sticks" and a big black support boot. Mary was a gracious hostess and attended to my every need. I was beholden. And, I was glad I had made the decision to accept her offer. Our lives together took on a nice rhythm immediately and I think my presence did her more good than it did me. She kept telling me she felt "useful." I worried, however, that having a man around might remind her too much about her life with Fred and wind up depressing her. It seemed to have the opposite effect.

We did the occasional errand together, watched TV together, and ate together although her cooking was not quite ready for prime time. I remembered her saying something days ago about "learning how to cook." We also gave each other space when that seemed right. I did some reading. She was downsizing and getting rid of clutter in anticipation of a move one day to a smaller place. So we went to our neutral corners and pretty much did our own thing.

I liked to sit on her deck and enjoy the afternoon sun. I saw Troy in his "Back 40" from time to time. But, no sign of Jenny or her showboat car. I mentioned it to Mary and she said that Jenny had not been around for a couple of days. She also said that she had made up her mind to drop Jenny as her realtor. She planned to tell her when she got back from wherever she was. In one way I wanted to be around when she did that. In another, I did not.

On the third day of my stay with Mary, Jeff

called. He was scheduled for surgery in two days. He sounded depressed. He wanted to stop by and say hello. I read that as his expecting to say good-bye. Mary invited him for lunch. He accepted, and she hummed happily as she got things ready. She's really been great.

The phone rang. I could hear her talking but not what she was saying. A few minutes later she came into the room to announce that Detective Ansini was going to join us after lunch. Surprise. He had called to say hello, and touch base on the Fred matter. Nothing new. She happened to mention that I was a house guest. He said that he was going to be in the neighborhood and asked if he might stop by and say hello. My new buddy.

Lunch with Jeff was uncomfortable. After the usual pleasantries. He was clearly depressed and disconsolate. We tried to cheer him up, but it didn't take. The conversation, and the anxiety that hovered over it, made Mary and me as uneasy.

He was focused on time. Time to live and time to die. Time to do what he wanted to do. Time to see his grandkids grow up. Time to win more time. He got almost darkly philosophical. "Time is not ours to give." he said. "Time is only something that is taken from us...like a burglar who sneaks in and takes the candlesticks leaving nothing behind but a dusty mark of where they once were."

It made me think of Jean Valjean and the silverware. It was depressing and emotional. Mary wiped away a tear trying to be inconspicuous. We all stared at the soup as silence became an increasingly uncomfortable part of the luncheon menu.

When the doorbell rang, it came as a relief to me, and I think to Mary. I think also to Jeff. I knew him and I was sure he knew he was depressing us. I think he was probably looking for a cue to leave. He had indicated earlier that he didn't want to get in the way of any conversation with Detective Ansini. He excused himself hurriedly and got up to leave.

He and Detective Ansini passed one another in the hallway. After brief introductions Jeff was gone. Ansini came in and the three of us chatted. I think Mary picked up that Ansini wanted to talk with me. She diplomatically excused herself to do the dishes.

Ansini and I went out on the deck. The sun felt good and we both savored it for a moment or two.

He began the conversation. "There have been some new developments in the Furman case."

"Oh."

"I can't really go in to detail, but I think there's going to be another hearing soon. All I can tell you is that it's going to be a doozy. There's a new investigation going on. The feds are involved. I think you'll be reading about it."

This was more than a little interesting to me. I leaned toward him hoping it would encourage more.

"I had a meeting with them, the feds, the other

day and I mentioned your name."

I was incredulous. "My name?"

"Nothing serious. I was asked about young Furman and how I got interested in him. I said you put a bee in my bonnet. That's all. I don't think there's a chance in hell that you'll be involved in any investigation I said you had concerns about undocumented workers. They're looking at the drugs, but I did want to let you know that your name's out there. I didn't want you to be sandbagged if anyone contacted you."

"Well thanks for that. But what else can you me about all of this? Is it what we thought, that Furman is likely to change his plea...look for a deal?"

"That's part of it, but I really can't tell you anything more. I can say that young Mark may just be the tip of the iceberg when it comes to the opioids...Fentanyl." That brought out a sly smile. "Who'd have thunk it?"

My curiosity level was way up there. I made a couple of other passes with no success. "When do you think I should start paying more attention to the papers?"

"Believe me, you'll know it when you see it." It was clear the conversation on the subject was over. I rocked in my chair. He enjoyed the sun.

"I have something else to tell you that I can't tell you much about, but I want your word that you won't say anything to your...eh... lady friend."

I chuckled. "Don't get the wrong idea about her and me. I'm too old for any of that stuff."

"I know. Just kidding." He waited for a response to his question. "Well?"

"Sure. I can keep a secret. What's all this about."

He moved toward me conspiratorially. With his lips near my ear he said, "I may have a way to get the little lady her death certificate."

"How the hell...?" He shushed me.

"You are full of surprises today," I said. "I've always understood that you pretty much need a body..."

"It's not one hundred percent." I could barely hear him. "But it just might work out. Keep it to yourself."

"Keep what to yourself?" Mary had just stepped onto the deck. I don't think she heard any of the earlier part of the conversation.

"Boy talk," said Ansini.

"He thinks you and I are an item...living in sin."

"Hah. If I were forty years younger, maybe we would be," she said. We all laughed just as the doorbell rang.

Ansini and I sat in silence. We could hear women's voices in the background. Unintelligible at first, only an occasional word made it out to the deck. The volume increased over several minutes. More of the conversation made its way to us. One word in particular came through loud and clear. The one word "bitch!" Then the front door slammed. A moment later, we could hear the roar of a powerful engine and the screeching of tires.

Ansini and I looked at each other, wondering what the hell's was going on? I thought I knew.

It was a minute or two later that Mary came out to us rubbing her hands. Her face was bright red.

"Well, that was something." She looked at me. "That was our neighbor, Jenny Hacker."

"Didn't sound like a friendly visit," I said.

Ansini sat silently with a puzzled look.

"She came to ask about selling the house again. We made small talk at first. She told me that her dog had been killed. Then that she and Troy had separated and would probably be getting a divorce. I thought she was just trying to get me to feel sorry for her so I'd sign up.

"Then she gave me her pitch again. It wasn't quite take it or leave it. More like we've gotta get this done, and get it done now.

"I told her that I was having second thoughts about that. She didn't take it well. She actually began to plead with me. She said her life was falling apart since her dog died...the divorce...going out on her own, and how much she really needed the business."

Getting a divorce I thought. I was right about that almost from the first time I saw the Troy-Jenny dynamic.

"When I told her that I definitely was not going to sign any contracts right now, she exploded."

"We heard," said Ansini. "Was that her car we heard blasting off?"

"Yeah. She was really angry." Mary turned to me. "Trav, I'm glad you're staying with me. I'm a little afraid of her. No telling what she might do. She is one angry lady. God, I hate confrontations like that."

Ansini stood up. "She'll cool off. If not, you know who to call."

Mary stood there shaking her head.

"I've got to go," said Ansini.

"I'll show you out," said Mary gesturing toward the door.

A minute or two later she came back and took Ansini's former seat.

I looked at her. She still looked shaken.

I reached over and took her hand. "Quite an afternoon!" I said.

"Can we go back to breakfast and start the day all over again?" A plaintive question.

"Can we go back to 1960 and start all over again?" It brought a trace of a smile.

We sat silently. I thought about the last two hours. Lunch with a friend who thought he was dying and very well might be. And a raging, screaming realtor who apparently was mourning a deceased dog first, and a doomed marriage second.

And, I could not cheer her up with the only positive of the last hour...the fact Ansini might come to her rescue with the insurance company.

I had to remain silent on that, and silently wondered whether I was somehow going to be drawn into the Furman saga. I also wondered what the new "doozy" development in that case was going to be?

My ankle was throbbing. An afternoon like this, I thought, isn't very therapeutic.

I was surprised when I was contacted by an agent from the DEA. His name was Berkowitz. He asked If I could come down for a brief "chat." I asked what it was all about and he played coy saying it was in connection with an ongoing investigation and not something he could discuss over the phone. I explained that I was not getting around very well and that it would be difficult for me to make the trip. He was insistent. Mary agreed to take me the next morning.

She remained in an outer office while I met with Berkowitz in a large conference room that seemed even larger with just two people sitting at a huge table that could have accommodated twenty people. I wondered how often there actually was a full house?

Berkowitz sat across from me. The window was at his back. Bright sunlight behind him made it difficult for me to see more than a silhouette.

It was disconcerting, like talking to Oz behind the curtain. This Oz had a legal pad in front of him, and a pencil in his hand.

He thanked me for coming and said that he just had a few questions concerning a current investigation. When I asked investigation of what, he told me it concerned "the Furman case."

"I don't know anything about the Furman case aside from what I read in the paper," I said.

The voice without a face said, "But you knew him didn't you?"

"I met him once. In his office."

"What was that all about?"

This was a tricky point for me. I had met Furman under false pretenses, pretending I was interested in a possible franchise. Not a crime, but it was awkward.

"I was interested in a possible landscaping company franchise."

"Oh. Somehow I was under the impression you thought his company might be running undocumented workers."

"Where did you get that idea?"

"Some of the people we're working with mentioned it."

"Ansini?"

The sun went behind a cloud and I could suddenly see the agent's face. He looked a little surprised but ignored the question.

"I'm just curious as to why you were so interested in the Furmans?"

He tapped the pencil in the palm of hand.

"Not the Furmans, plural, just Mark Furman."

"But you went to the hearing...the Mark Furman hearing didn't you? Why?"

"Just curious. Old guys like me sometimes go to the courthouse for the fun of it. It's better than television. Sometimes."

"That was about drugs." More pencil play. "Did you ever have any reason to suspect that he might be dealing?"

"No."

"Did you ever have contact with Mark Furman Senior?"

"No. Is he involved?"

"I can't get into that Mr. McGee. As I say, it's the early part of an investigation."

He disappeared in the bright backlight once again and asked a few more questions about my all but non-existent relationship with Mark Furman. The conversation didn't seem to give him anything useful. I didn't see him make any notes.

After about twenty minutes he thanked me for coming and told me I was "free to go."

I struggled to get up and manage my sticks. He stood as if he were going to offer to help, but he didn't.

"You know," I said, "this has been a colossal waste of time for me. I don't know why you might think I could be of any possible use to you and this investigation. Look at me. I've got a bum ankle. It's hard to get around. I had to get someone to drive me. Couldn't this have been handled over the phone?"

"I'm sorry Mr. McGee. But with a case involving people like the Furmans...it's delicate...we don't like to use the phones. And I, personally, like to talk to people face to face. Gives me a better read on who's telling the truth." His tone and expression were infuriatingly patronizing. I wanted to smack him with one of my crutches. Undoubtedly that's a federal offense.

"I hope I passed your friggin' test," I said in disgust as I turned toward the door. He did not comment. Nor did he thank me for coming. Nor did he say goodbye.

But as I left I knew that I was leaving with more than I had come with. Mr. Agent Berkowitz had slipped. He had made a mistake that could probably earn him a demerit from the bosses in this confidential investigation. He had referred more than once to the Furmans. He had said "in a case involving the Furmans" plural, not Furman singular.

In my mind that means that it was not only Mark Furman Junior who was targeted or if interest in the investigation, but that apparently, Mark Furman Senior was also. Now Ansini's "doozy" comment came into shaper focus. And, if both Furmans were involved in drugs, it would...in this town...be a doozy indeed. This would be a good time to have that beer with Ansini.

We had just opened the door on our return to Mary's place when I heard my cell phone chirping. Once again, I had forgotten it when we went downtown. I'll have to work on that. It was right where I left it on the kitchen table. I read the name Carr. But it was William Carr...not Jeff. I answered with some trepidation.

"Mr. McGee. My name's Bill Carr...Jeff's son." He sounded a lot like Jeff.

"We've never met, but feel that I know you. Dad talks about you a lot. He wanted me to call."

"Please call me Trav, Bill. Is anything wrong?" My pulse quickened. Jeff was scheduled for surgery tomorrow.

"Well, yes, and no, and I don't know. Things are kind of mixed up. Dad was operated on this morning."

"Today? I thought it was scheduled for tomorrow."

"They pushed it up a day." He took a deep breath. "They did a biopsy. Cancer. So, they decided to move sooner rather than later.

"They performed a hepatectomy...I think that's what they called it. He came out of the surgery okay, but he's not out of the woods by a long shot." The words stung. I remembered my Holly. They basically opened her up, took a look at what was a hopeless case, and closed her. The cancer had won uncontested...without a fight. I could not and would not mention Holly to Carr...either Carr.

"They lifted a pretty good sized tumor from his liver. The question now, is did they get it all? Has it spread? It's too early for any of that. It doesn't sound good. But there are some positives. At least they could get at it. When the cancer's advanced, they usually can't. People survive liver cancer...cut a piece out...and the liver may regrow...regenerate." He took another deep breath.

"Oh, the poor guy. I'm so sorry he's dealing with this...that you're dealing with it."

"I'm at the hospital now awaiting the next word from the doctors. The really bad news is we're dealing with cancer...liver cancer. The survival rate's not good. It doesn't get much worse than that. Lots of questions ahead."

I was stunned, deflated. I was filled with dread, remembering Holly's diagnosis and death. A flurry of other thoughts tumbled through my mind in milliseconds. The news was so sudden and so dramatic. I had been hoping that this was something his doctors would be able to deal with...that the shadows or spots they'd found were something they could manage.

I thought about spending the morning in that stupid meeting with Berkowitz...wasting that time...when I might have been at the hospital near my friend while he was being operated on. It was something I had intended to do tomorrow.

Bill Carr's voice brought me back. "As I say, he's resting comfortably and we're waiting to hear more. He wanted me to be sure to get to you as soon as it was over regardless..."

"Bill, I wanted to be there. I'm sorry. I didn't know the surgery had been moved up." He said something I could not understand. "Shall I come by. Is there anything I can do for you?"

His voice was different. I could not tell if he was tired or if he was weeping. "Thanks. No. He's out and will be for several hours. I'm just going to wait here until the docs get back to me. My wife's with me. We'll just wait it out. I'll get back to you when I have any news." He took a deep breath.

"And Trav...thanks for being dad's friend. It meant...I mean...it *means* a lot to him."

"Bill, I'm just devastated. I've got my prayer beads out and my fingers crossed that the news will be good."

We thanked each other once again and he repeated his promise to call whenever there was anything to report and he could tell me when I might visit my friend.

It put the revelation I had learned, or believe I had learned about the Furmans earlier in the day on the back burner. It was an interesting twist, but aside from being an interested observer, I had no role to play. Like everyone else, I'd just watch it play out. I didn't really care. In a way, it was the same with Jeff. I had no role to play in what lay ahead for him. I could only let it play out. The difference was that I did care. I really did care. The Furmans, junior, or senior, or both be damned.

I went to bed sad, wondering what the next day or days held, and thinking of my friend in a post surgical stupor hooked to tubes and machines in an antiseptic and impersonal hospital room with anonymous people attending. Should I dare to be hopeful?

I was allowed to visit Jeff two days later. Doctors were optimistic and everyone was in a brighter mood though recovery was going to take some time and there was always the possibility of setbacks.

Jeff looked like hell, but he'd just been through hell. He was weak. His color was not much better than the sheets surrounding him. His voice was faint. I was allowed to spend only a few minutes with him. We did not talk too much. It seemed to take a lot out of him. I left uncertain. All I could do was hope that things were on the right track. I wanted to be optimistic. It was a challenge.

Bill Carr and his wife proved a lovely couple who'd obviously been worn down by everything that was going on. Apparently Bill and his wife had had an emotional conversation with Jeff about implementing his advanced directive. "He reminded me about it," said Bill. "We agreed to put all that on hold because of the doctor's optimism. He told me in no uncertain terms though, that if things take a turn for the worse, he wants the DNR implemented. The doctor understands and that's a relief to dad."

So, it's come to that, I thought. How sad. We chatted briefly about other things. They were grateful I'd come by. I promised to come back soon.

There was no opportunity...and no real desire...to talk about the big story in the morning paper. They all had other things on their minds.

The Furman story was out. The newspaper article quoted "informed sources" and "sources close to the investigation" which is newspeak for leaked information. The story ran under the headline "Civic Leader and Son Under Apparent Investigation in Opioid Scheme." There it was for all to see.

Local civic leader Mark Furman, Sr. and his son Mark Furman, Jr. are under investigation for possible involvement in distribution of the opioid Fentanyl and other drugs, according to informed sources.

The Drug Enforcement Agency refuses to acknowledge an investigation, but according to sources familiar with the alleged probe, the father-son team has been importing opioids, and possibly other drugs, from Mexico.

Furman, Sr. is the president of National American Landscaping, a company that franchises local landscaping companies in six states. His son is vice president of the company.

A large quantity of Fentanyl was seized at the company office and from the Furman home in the county earlier this week. No charges have yet been filed, but our sources close to the investigation say warrants are likely within the next days.

No dollar value has been placed on the scope of the alleged operation.

Attempts to reach the Furmans for comment have been unsuccessful.

The younger Furman was recently arrested with several other men on drunk and disorderly charges following an altercation at Barney's Bistro on Lombard St. All were also charged with disorderly conduct and possession of drugs. One of the men, who was not identified, faces an illegal firearms charge.

Furman has pleaded not guilty. Attempts to reach his attorney, Maurice Dowd, have been unsuccessful.

Sources tell us that the Furmans allegedly acquired the drugs from contacts in Mexico, one of the world's largest producers of illegal Fentanyl, and from an unidentified out of state drug compounding company.

The news is expected to send shock waves through the civic and political communities. The elder Furman is a member of several non-

profit boards and a close friend of, and donor to, many politicians including the governor, the mayor and other political office-holders past and present.

Allison Manor, Mayor Joseph Allenby's press secretary says the mayor is "dismayed" over the alleged investigation but refused further comment. Requests for comment from other local officials have been unsuccessful.

The opioid epidemic has been a priority of the Allenby administration in view of the growing number of deaths in this community. The opioid-related death toll has risen sharply in recent years taking 1,500 lives in the past year.

This reporter has been told that the investigation into the operation has been conducted by a task force comprised of federal and local law enforcement personnel. The Drug Enforcement Unit of the Metropolitan Police Department refuses to comment on it or how it might be involved.

Attempts to learn further details on the scope of the alleged investigation have been unsuccessful.

I was surprised to see the story in print. In a sense it didn't seem fair. The reporter didn't have anything in the way of corroboration beyond informed sources. The lid was on all around. "No comment"…"alleged" this and that. I wondered who would have leaked the story and why. The best I could come up with was that someone wanted to shake the tree and see what fell. I could see that kind of tactic from someone like Agent Berkowitz. I could also see a lawsuit in play unless some formal charge was filed, and filed soon.

The television and radio stations were having a "breaking news" frenzy doing what they do best; taking a newspaper story and running with it as if it were their own. No one was able to pry any more information or comment than the newspaper already had. There were a bunch of "no comments" from barely recognizable people who lived on the periphery of power and influence. A few television types found relevant locations to offer breathless faux earnest characterizations of "blockbuster allegations" covering their inability to advance the story. Been there and done that I thought.

One pretty reporter stood outside the Furman home but could manage no more information than the fact she had no information. She made a big thing over the fact no lights were on in the house. There'd be no Emmy awarded for the day's coverage.

The few radio stations that even had newscasts simply carried stories written directly from the newspaper article.

I moved back into my place the next day. My ankle was far from healed, but I was able to get around a lot better with my crutches and big black boot. Driving was not in the picture, but Mary...probably in self defense...had helped me download an app for Uber. If I needed to get anywhere I could manage that way. She had opened up a whole new world for me by introducing me to the app universe. I got to thinking my phone might be worth the monthly bill after all.

I got a call from Bill Carr telling me that it was still wait and see at the hospital. Doctors were concerned, as they always are when it comes to the liver, about bleeding and other post operative issues. "It's going to be a long haul," he told me. "Ten days or so in the hospital, then a couple of months additional recovery. If he gets through that, he's still fighting survival odds. We'll just have to wait and see." I didn't tell him that my Holly never got those "couple of months."

He was going to have to leave and return home for a while. He was involved in some law enforcement matters that required his presence at a deposition.

"I know I don't have to ask this Trav, but I'd appreciate it if you would stop in from time to time. He's pretty down."

He didn't have to ask, and I promised I'd be there.

DENEISHA

The pressure was on. The Furman story had awakened a sleeping giant; the public. Most of the blue ribbon civic and political leaders remained in their bunkers, but the next day, something spontaneous erupted. The fact the focus of the Furman accusation was on opioids woke up a lot of people. While leaders of respected organizations remained silent, individual members and other citizens did not. Voice was given to smaller neighborhood organizations. Drugs had long been a scourge in black community. Opioids and the resurgence of heroin were hitting hard. In more affluent populations, opioid use was a newer kind of threat taking young lives of middle and upper class kids. Parents could wink at pot use but not at the newest crisis. Opioids were different.

People were angry and making demands that the epidemic be brought under control. What quickly emerged was a collaboration of concern among disparate groups. Suddenly, formerly anonymous spokespeople were appearing on television, radio, and capturing newspaper headlines demanding that something be done about the problem, and that the Furmans be locked up. It was a guilty until proven innocent atmosphere.

The mob wanted scalps, and Furman Senior and Junior, still not convicted of anything, found themselves the target of everything. They too were deep in some bunker somewhere undoubtedly realizing that a public appearance would be at their personal peril.

This loose confederation had a common goal, but not a common leader. At least not initially. One emerged very quickly. It was spontaneous combustion. Her name was DeNeisha Trotter aka DeNasty...the prosecutor.

While other political leaders were silent, she was anything but. She was perfect for the task. She had what many were calling "chops." She was a dedicated crime fighter. She had clout. She was impassioned and articulate. She was a woman. She was black. She was strikingly telegenic. She was committed to the cause. She was also politically ambitious.

Her commitment was not solely the result of political expedience. She had grown up poor, in one the northern big cities, in one of the many ethnically mixed neighborhoods where street crime dominated daily life, and drugs were the common denominator. Her brother had been gunned down in a drive-by outside her home.

She was first to the body, alone with him long enough to pry a plastic packet from his dead hand. She was street wise enough to know what it was. She hid it in her jeans as she waited for the cops. It was not a long wait as sirens were shrieking in the distance and closing within minutes of the shooting.

Officers did not move quite as quickly as they went about the familiar routine of seeking answers and getting none from sullen neighborhood residents. Onlookers mumbled angrily in English and Spanish as officers completed the all too familiar task of processing yet another victim of the street wars. They did so with one eye on the victim and the other on the restive neighbors.

In those tear-filled moments of sorrow and confusion, DeNeisha made a decision that would change her life. As officers prepared to leave, she called over a sergeant and handed him the packet of drugs.

"Found it near the body," she said.

The officer took the plastic bag. He and DeNeisha stared at other suspiciously. He wrestled over whether to take her in for further questioning. He knew she was the dead boy's sister. She wondered if she had done the right thing. He pulled out a handkerchief, and gently wiped away her tears.

"Thanks," he said softly. "Now you go home and be a good girl. Your parents need you."

DeNeisha Trotter decided then and there that she would one day leave those streets and become something; somebody. And, that's exactly what she did with a lot of help from her mother, her minister, her teachers and a better than average mind that won her a scholarship to Northwestern and Yale Law. DeNeisha Trotter was an exception in her neighborhood in more ways than one. She broke out, mindful from that day forward of those who did not and could not.

When she realized that something was bringing residents of her city together after the Furman story broke, she knew she could take advantage of the situation. It could help the city, and if along the way it helped her, that would be all right too. But she knew should would have to navigate these new waters very carefully. There were some very important toes she could not afford to step on. And, she also had to be careful with the feds. They had toes too, and if the case proceeded as it appeared it might, it would be their baby. She would have to be something of a midwife on the sidelines.

She held a televised news conference to proclaim her determination to make drug prosecutions a priority, and announced her intention to establish a special unit in the prosecutor's office to deal with drug cases and issues. She promised to work with community leaders in all communities on drug awareness and education. She made an impassioned appeal for city politicians, police and civic leaders to join the effort. No doubt, the image of her dead brother crossed her mind as she spoke.

She and her entourage faced a barrage of questions from reporters. DeNeisha refused to get involved in the Furman allegations, saying they were just that, "allegations" and that the father and son were entitled to their day in court if it came to that. If it did, she promised a rigorous prosecution if the case came to her, although she believed the feds would probably have jurisdiction...again...if they were prosecuted at all.

She was surrounded by a contingent of representatives of neighborhood organizations and activist groups. They shouted enthusiastic approval and waved crude signs proclaiming their anger and demands as she spoke. They wanted justice and they wanted it quickly.

Their emotion fueled her. She issued a challenge that sounded more like a demand for the political powers to step forward and join her commitment to deal with the opioid crisis saying, "We don't have to identify the threat, we have to eliminate it...and it takes all of us to do it. All of us Mr. Mayor...Ms. Council President...Mr. Police Chief. All of us!"

Her entourage applauded with sustained enthusiasm. The TV cameras rolled. The challenge had been issued. Pity the poor public servant or civil leader who did not rise to it. DeNeisha Trotter had spoken and was at the top of her game.

They watched separately

Trav McGee watched with a broad smile. He liked her style.

Detective Paul Ansini watched nodding approval throughout, thinking so what if she were politically ambitious and playing to that ambition. She was doing the right thing.

Agents Berkowitz and Dougherty watched, happy to have an ally who could marshal pubic support. Each thought she was a good ally as long as she didn't get in the way or steal any thunder.

Mark Furman Senior and Junior watched more fearful than ever of what the near future held for them.

Jeff Carr watched with tears in his eyes.

Troy Hacker didn't much care. He had his own issues.

Jenny Hacker watched in a bar with friends. The TV was on but she wasn't paying attention.

Mary Haller missed it altogether. She was busy removing clutter.

News directors and editors knew they had their lede for the evening broadcasts and for the next day's edition.

FURMAN SENIOR, AND JUNIOR

The two Furmans sat silently at the breakfast table reading the morning paper on their phones. Each picked at his food, fearful of looking at the other. The story was big. The DeNeisha Trotter news conference took up most of the front page, complete with a huge picture showing her pointing an accusing finger toward the reader, presumably at the moment she was challenging city officials to carry their weight in dealing with the opioid epidemic.

They finished at about the same time without comment. Any observer would have concluded that neither wanted to be in the presence of the other. They would have been correct. Mrs. Furman apparently didn't want to either. She had left for a visit with her cousin on the other side of the state.

At the moment, both men were awaiting the arrival of federal agents who had very politely requested a meeting to discuss "recent events." Furman Senior had taken the call. Though informal, each was invited to bring along his attorney. The meeting would be downtown. As a courtesy, the caller offered to send a car for them. He "understood their desire to avoid public appearances at this time." The mood was such that confrontation would be inevitable and potentially violent.

The senior Furman went to the window and peered through the blinds. "Still out there," he muttered to himself as reporters mingled just beyond the lawn and their property line.

His son shook his head. "How do we get out of here without having to deal with them?" He stood and paced as his father took another look out the window.

"We can't," he snapped. "That's why they're coming to get us. They'll take us downtown for the interview."

"That'll give them some nice pictures of us being hauled away. They should talk to us here."

"They wouldn't be talking to us at all you stupid queer, if you hadn't gotten into that jam at the bar and caught everyone's attention."

The words stung. The younger Furman's shoulders slumped as they always did when his father got on him. That was something that had been happening for most of his life, especially since he came out as a teenager. It was less his coming out voluntarily, than his father suspecting as much and challenging him to deny it.

It was a painful confession and Mark Senior had lost few opportunities to humiliate him in all the years since. That did not extend to his willingness to take him on at the company. It was not a case of blood being thicker than water. It was for protection, for his son had learned of the sideline he was working through National American. Had Mark been stronger, he could have used that leverage to even the playing table in their relationship. Much stronger was his desire to escape. Escape the home. Escape the daily proximity to his father. Escape a job he hated. He needed to bankroll that escape and to move on to the kind of good life he'd imagined all his life, but live it on his own terms. To do that, he had to become involved in his father's sideshow.

It had been a costly weakness. He had fallen in with some bad company and gotten into something a lot deeper than recreational drugs. Worst of all he'd had the very bad drug-induced judgment to tell G.G. Goodstrich about his father's extra-curricular activity.

Then there was his sexual relationship with G.G. and others. Goodstrich was not exactly black-mailing him. But he been coming to him for so called "loans" often; more and more often recently. Often enough that Mark could not afford to take off, break free, and end the painfully and dreadfully humiliating life at home and office. It was a life in which his father, who hated him, wanted him close where he could maintain control of and protective of his business interests; all of his business interests.

The last time G.G. "requested" such a loan, Mark resisted. G.G. suggested, more forcefully than he ever had before, that he knew how to let the right people "downtown" know about "dear old dad." The next thing he knew, punches were being thrown, and landing, at that brawl that he now marked as the beginning of what was very likely the end.

Now he had to meet with federal agents who were eager to hear the formal version of his story. Dowd would be with him. But young Mark knew that they knew that he had damaging, even explosive details to add.

His father had not formally connected all the dots, but he was extraordinarily nervous and agitated after the newspaper article and television reports implied in no uncertain terms that father and son were the subject of a federal investigation. The city was in an angry mood and that prosecutor was making sure it stayed that way.

He was trapped and not unmindful of the irony that his downfall came as a result of trying to protect the father he had come to hate.

Mark Furman Senior didn't know details of the story that was about to overwhelm him and that his son was a Judas. He did know he was vulnerable now, extremely exposed thanks to his son's carelessness. The newspaper article and the DeNeisha Trotter news conference had made it clear. If Mark Junior had not gotten into the brawl at the bar, there would have been no investigation.

He didn't know that his son's lawyer's conversation with federal agents had triggered the demand to meet with both of them that morning. He asked himself what federal agents could know that would bring his name into it? Having that name in the same sentence with a son facing a drug charge was enormously threatening and distressful.

It had all started when Mark Junior was in college and far removed from his father's "other" business. He was glad to have his gay kid out of the house and out of state. The business was doing well. The labor supply was good. Franchise interest was high. There were occasional immigration issues but they were handled through exchanges between attorneys. It was suggested that he should fly to Mexico City and establish a personal relationship with a lawyer named Angel. Turns out he was no angel but rather a shady character with cartel connections and all that came with it.

He met the Mexican in an impressive building in downtown Mexico City. It was lavishly appointed with artwork Furman recognized as Italian and expensive. Though Mexican, Angel more or less fit the same description. His expensively styled black hair was long, spilled over the back of his collar, and was accented with streaks of white. He had the face and complexion of a campesino and was dressed for success, complete with five thousand dollar suit, white shirt and silver tie. A gold tooth was conspicuous between thick wet lips. A gold Rolex peeked out from starched French cuffs. His hands were working class but his nails indicated time well spent on the receiving end of an attentive attendant's skills, no doubt at a comfortable high-end salon.

Angel had a proposition. It was proposed in flawless English Godfather language as one he believed Furman "could not refuse." Angel presented it in business terms, calling it a "business deal" involving the "outsourcing" of Mexican Fentanyl to "commercial partners" in the "Estados Unidos."

Outraged at first, Furman listened and learned that Angel had a completely workable deal facilitated by certain people with the kind of credentials that eased travel between the two countries. Angel explained that he was attracted by the Midwestern reach of Furman's company. He would leave it up to Furman to organize the next step in the distribution process. The Mexicans wanted "fifty" cents on the dollar for "product." Prices would be established by "market conditions".

"Receive, distribute collect," crooned Angel. "It's that easy.

The earlier outrage disappeared and Furman was in. They also made a little side deal about providing laborers for the Furman company. Angel had access to guest worker visas and could shuttle workers in and out of the U.S. at will. Just in emergencies of course. And, at a price to be negotiated. Furman wondered if the men Angel might send North might also be called "product." He didn't care. The conversation never got that far. As Angel said, "just consider this discussion a 'memorandum of understanding' on that."

As Furman Senior waited for the agents to arrive, he remembered that he had thought the deal with the Mexican seemed elegant in its simplicity. A can't miss deal. At the time. But, where is Angel now when he really needed him?

"They'll be here in three hours," he said quietly as if talking to himself. His son did not respond.

"I'd give a lot to know how my name got into this." His voice was a little stronger. It was something he had wondered about since the avalanche of newspaper articles and all the publicity had overwhelmed him.

There was no response from his son.

"Your man Dowd talked to these guys didn't he? What did he tell you about them? What did he say to you?"

This was a conversation young Mark dreaded. He always knew it would come one day. He feared it as he feared his father's uncanny ability to read him almost to the point of knowing what he was thinking. It would have been much easier if his mother had stayed at home. She was the firewall between him and his father. He'd often found refuge there behind that wall. Now she was gone, and like a Joshua circling with his ram's horns, his father threatened that sanctuary's protective wall.

"I don't really know much about it." He did not look at his father as he spoke.

"What? You're telling me your attorney talked to federal agents about you and you and he have not talked? Incredible."

Mark could feel the warmth of a flush. His underarms were wet. "I don't know."

His father paced, lightly striking the palm of one hand with a fist from his other. Back and forth, back and forth. With a sudden turn toward his son that surprised Mark, he blurted, "What was Dowd doing talking to them in the first place?" He paused for a few seconds. "Your case is local, not federal."

Mark shifted in his chair. He began to tremble and couldn't make eye contact with his father who now hovered over him, his fists clenched. "Well, why the hell was Dowd talking to the feds?" He began to pace again, giving Mark Junior a little more welcome space. He could feel the heat coming from his father's form even from a few feet away.

"I think I finally get it," he said, turning once again toward his son. "You son of a bitch. You're looking for a deal!"

The younger Furman sagged even further in his chair. Here it was. His worst fear. He wanted to be far, far away from when his father finally realized what was going on. Impossible now. It was one on one. No firewall.

"You know you don't have a leg to stand on in state court. We all know what happens to sissies when the prison gate shuts. Then, all of a sudden, a story pops up in the paper linking the two of us in a drug operation...a drug ring...after your man Dowd talks to the feds." He pointed a shaking finger at his son. "One and one makes two. I can't believe it took me this long to figure it out."

Mark was shaking more visibly now, still looking anywhere but in the direction of his father. He did not respond.

"Look at you sitting there, shaking like a fucking leaf. I'm right aren't I? How much do they know?"

No response.

His father shouted. "I'm right aren't I.! Goddammit! How much did you...or Dowd...tell them?"

"Stop it! Stop it!" Mark was screaming. "I didn't tell them anything. I told you, I haven't talked to them."

"Of course not. You don't have the balls. Your lawyer does. He told them about the Fentanyl didn't he? Of course he did and now the feds want to have a nice, quiet chat before slapping on the handcuffs. Nice going," he said sarcastically. "Nice going. And thanks. I should have known you'd blow it...that one way or another, you'd fuck it up." He shook his head. "Shame on me. I should have known." He turned from Mark. "I should have known," he said kicking at a chair.

There were tears in young Mark Furman's eyes as he watched his father slump into another chair. He was weeping, not for his father's distress, but for his own. His father knew of his betrayal, and he knew his father hated him more than ever for the chain of events he had unleashed, just as he knew that when the chain was completed, he and his father would be spending a long time behind bars.

"Cellmates," he laughed the word. "Cellmates. Maybe we'll be cellmates. Wouldn't you love that?" By now he was both laughing and crying.

His father turned. His face was turning purple, deformed with rage. His breathing was labored and loud.

"Of course I'm going to tell them." His voice rose in crescendo as if directed by an enthusiastic maestro. "Of course I want a deal. Of course I don't give a crap about you just as you have never given one shit about me. Wouldn't you do the same thing?" He pointed a shaking finger at the older man. "You'd turn on me in a heartbeat. You've turned on me all of my life." His voice showed a rage of its own; a simmering fury.

"Why you bastard..." shouted his father grabbing his chest. It felt as if it was about to explode.

Both men went quiet except for the labored breathing, sounding like two pugilists at the end of a furious round. Like fighters they had thrown verbal punches designed to hurt and destroy, and were now momentarily in their respective corners.

Mark Furman Senior got up slowly, his hand still on his chest. He left the room, a wounded and defeated man. He said nothing as the door shut quietly behind him. His son followed him out with his eyes. In a strange way, he felt relieved...relieved at having finally removed a heavy burden... that he had not let his father win once again...that it was Mark Furman Senior who had retreated. Not he. For once in his relationship with his father, he thought, he had won a victory. He was, for once, feeling a sense of proud confidence rather than humiliation. Yes, he thought, it was a victory. Given what lay ahead, a Pyrrhic victory perhaps, but victory nonetheless.

He was turning for a glass of water when he heard the door behind him open. He turned. He barely had time to grasp what he was seeing. The instant he began to comprehend that his father was holding a gun, the gun exploded and Mark Furman's life ended.

He never heard the second shot.

Reporters outside the house were chatting amongst themselves when one of them said, "What was that." Their eyes turned toward the house, then back toward each other.

"There it is again. It sounded like a shot...or shots," said one of the young men to a colleague.

"You sure?"

"Uh-huh."

"Whatever it was, it sure sounded like it came from the house."

"Maybe they're having a fart contest," shouted one trying to be funny.

As the others stood in uncertainty, an attractive young television reporter said, "Let's find out. She walked hesitatingly toward the house, climbed the stairs and rang the bell. Her colleagues watched as she waited.

There was no answer.

MCGEE

I t was a media firestorm. The evening news was dominated by word of the apparent murder suicide of the Furmans.

I could hardly believe it when the reports started to come in at mid-afternoon. It dawned on me as the news unfolded that I had played a role in early events that led to the two deaths. I had talked to Ansini about the possibility of undocumented workers. I visited young Furman. Ansini did as well. The arrest of Mark Furman Junior piqued our interest and also caught the attention of the feds who flexed their muscles. I assumed it was the brace of DEA agents who had leaked the story about the Furmans being included in a major investigation that led to the bloody discovery in the Furman kitchen. Yet, if I had had any role at all in the sequence of events, I had to take it one step backward. It really all started with the flap over the Hacker landscape project and Fred Haller.

Fred, after all, had raised the possibility of undocumented workers involved in that project. It was, indeed, a tangled web.

Technically, the events surrounding the double shooting were still subject to investigation. However no one doubted that it was indeed a murder-suicide in which the elder Furman killed his son and then himself and that it was likely connected to the drug allegations that had received so much publicity.

The television stations covered it the way television stations do. Video of ambulances and police vehicles outside the Furman home now circled with crime-scene tape was replayed again and again. Shocked neighbors were interviewed. The two Furmans were remembered as fine, upstanding people and wonderful neighbors. Some dismissed the allegations about their alleged involvement with drugs, of which there would be constant reminders, on television and in the newspaper. Others believed the shootings confirmed illegal activity on the part of both Furman Senior and Junior.

I found it amusing to watch and read about city officials briefly coming out of their bunkers like Punxsutawney Phil to express televised dismay. Like the loveable groundhog seeing its shadow, the politicians and civic leaders scurried back into burrows fearing the sudden burst of sunlight would reveal their close association with

Mark Furman Senior. For it seemed quite likely now that this pillar of the community...their friend and sometimes benefactor...was involved in the reported drug trafficking. Time for them to put some distance between them and the Furmans.

Attempts at comment from investigators into the allegations produced little beyond the promise that the investigation would continue.

The newspaper had a more detailed take on events than the television and radio reportage. It noted that continuing the investigation would be considerably more difficult without the principals in the alleged trafficking. The newspaper had learned that the double shooting had occurred just hours before the Furmans were scheduled to be interviewed by federal agents. That lent further credibility to the earlier allegations.

Mrs. Furman had been reached at a relative's home on the other side of the state. She was in shock, but before shutting down, she angrily denied that her husband and son had knowledge of any drug activity.

The attorney, Dowd, had little to say. True to his late client to the end, he would offer only that Furman Junior was innocent of any drug related crime and that he had been prepared to cooperate fully with any investigation before his father killed him.

The news cycle had moved on when, a few

days later, I received a call from Mary Haller. She was in a happy mood.

"I've sold the house." She almost sang the words as she repeated them. "Jenny or no Jenny, the place has been sold." Needless to say it was good news.

"That's wonderful Mary. How did you pull that off? It couldn't have been on the market more than a few days."

"Well, you heard about Jenny didn't you?"

"What about her?"

"She was killed...an auto accident."

"I had no idea. What happened?

"It happened the night those people were killed. The Furmans. She was apparently coming home late after a Mimosa party with the girls. Cops say she had that big red car of hers up to about a hundred when a tree got in the way." She took a deep breath. "I'm sorry to put it that way. But she was a bitch."

"Wow. That's a shocker. She was a piece of work but didn't deserve an end like that. Or deserve an end at all. She couldn't have been more than thirty two or so."

"She was thirty-four."

"Well, she wasn't going to sell your house anyway, was she?"

"No. I never signed a contract with her. But these realtors are something else. One of the ladies in her office apparently knew that Jenny had been working on me..."

"Her own company?" I interrupted.

"Her old office I guess. Anyway, she called, came over, said she thought she had someone who'd be just right for my house." She chuckled. "And she did. And at a good price. They're from California...sold a small house for a lot...and they're pre-approved. Voila. Sold!" She said it with a chord of triumph.

"So, what now."

"Looks like I'm finally going to get to move to Florida. And, I'm going to do it soon. Claudia...that's the realtor...says her clients want to move quickly. I could have a check in my hands by next week." She was all but humming.

"Sounds great."

I was trying to find the right way to put a question I felt the need to ask for a couple of reasons. All along I had been hopeful that Mary could put the disappearance of her husband behind her. Time had helped but earlier conversations, even recent ones, had convinced me that she was far from over it. I also knew that Ansini had indicated he might be able to get a Fred Haller death certificate. I had no idea what his insurance policy was worth, but that, the house sale and any retirement income she had would likely give her a comfortable life. I hoped so.

"What about Fred and the insurance? I think the question caught her off guard.

"Well, I can't wait here forever. Now I can afford to move."

Her words became very measured "I've accepted the fact long since that Fred's undoubtedly dead. One of these days, the insurance company will have to pay. I hope I live so long, but I can't let that be my life. It's time to move on. I'll stay in touch with Detective Ansini and we'll see where that goes."

We chatted about odds and ends and promised to get together one last time before she left town for Florida, becoming reacquainted with old friends and beginning a new life. I was sad. And happy. Her personality had changed with the house sale. She seemed as lighthearted and buoyant as I remembered from the television days. It was a far cry from her mood when she called to ask me for help.

That call also brought me peripherally into a series of events that in and of themselves that had nothing to do with Mary. It brought me into the world of Detective Ansini and even the Furmans. It had been an interesting time, giving an old man lots to think about and things to do. My life had become a little more interesting. Not quite like living on Travis McGee's houseboat in Fort Lauderdale, but interesting enough. He made a living doing interesting things. Oh well, you can't win 'em all.

For me, the next interesting thing was to visit

my friend Jeff Carr. He was still at the hospital but was doing well enough for doctors to be talking about going home. He'd need help when did. I intend to provide it. Interesting, he'd be coming back into my life at about the same time Mary Haller would be leaving it.

With Mary's imminent departure, I decided it was a good time to contact Ansini and press the death certificate issue. It had been several days since he teased me on that and had left me dangling. But, they had been some days for all of us. I would have to believe that he was involved in the Furman case, not to mention the trafficking situation. I hoped he could find time for me and that he could find it before Mary headed south.

I called him and left a message. When we finally connected I reminded him that we still had to sit down and have that beer together. I even said I would buy, although, I kidded, I was "on a fixed income." He got a laugh out of that and promised to get back. He said he was involved in the early stages of a mini task force investigation into the opioid traffic following the Furman saga. It told me it was complicated and international but would say no more.

I told him Mary Haller was leaving town, and I was curious about what he'd said about clearing the death certificate hurdle. He joked that I was trying to bribe him with a beer. He sure had loosened up since our first "five minutes."

His call came two days later. He said there was a pause in the action as far as his current activity was concerned. A good time to get together. We agreed to meet at Nellie's early in the afternoon when it was less crowded. I got there first and chose a corner table for privacy. I didn't have to wait long. He came in wearing a big smile. I watched him and Andy dip their chins in recognition. It was the first time. Ansini had joined the club on his third visit.

"What are you so happy about?" I asked.

"I've got a few hours to call my own. My colleagues are hung up in depositions on another case. So, here I am."

Nellie took our orders.

"How's the drug thing going?" I asked knowing he was not going to tell me very much about an active investigation.

"You know better than that." I thought that was it. He looked at me strangely as if he were deciding whether to give me more; whether he could trust me. To my surprise he went on.

"I can tell you this...and you've got to keep this under your hat...it's going better than we thought it would after the Furmans, eh...dropped out of the picture, shall we say. Our friend G.G. Goodstrich as it turns out, had a deeper relationship with Mark

Furman Junior than we knew. And, he knows a lot more about the Furman drug world than anyone thought. And, he's singing to save his ass."

Nellie brought our drinks. We stopped talking until she was out of earshot.

"That's all I can say. But it does give us an avenue to proceed on we didn't think we'd have after the Furmans died. Nuff said." He looked at me earnestly. "Keep it to yourself. Got it?"

I nodded. He wasn't kidding.

He changed the subject.

"By the way, I want to thank you."

I could feel my eyebrows climb. "For what?"

"For introducing me to Travis McGee...the other Travis McGee."

"I don't get it."

"When we first met, you told me that you called yourself Trav after the MacDonald character."

I had forgotten that.

He went on. "I like to read when I have the time. So, I picked up a couple of his books. They're hard to find, you know. He stopped writing more than thirty years ago."

"You should have asked me. I have them all."

"When I finish the ones I have maybe I can borrow a couple. I'm really enjoying them. He was quite a guy. A stud."

"That's just one way where we differ." I laughed and he did too.

"Anyway, thanks for tipping me off to Mac-Donald." He took a big swallow of his beer. "It helps me take my mind off the business at hand."

"No family?" I was surprised when I asked how little I knew about this man I had come to know, yet not know.

"No. Never happened." He looked reflective. "I can't tell you why exactly. No time maybe. I've always been too busy I guess. And I'm a loner at heart" He shrugged his shoulders. "Never met the right woman and all of that."

I had the impression he was not comfortable talking about himself. He was a guy, after all, who spent a career asking questions, not answering them. He seemed eager to change the subject.

"What about you?"

I told him my story. He seemed moved when I told him about the loss Jennifer and Holly. I included more detail than I intended. It gave me the realization that a good cop has the ability to get people to talk even when they don't want or intend to. If that was something you could learn I wish I had learned it as a reporter.

"So much pain," he said. "Maybe that's a good reason to go it alone. No one else to worry about. No one else to grieve."

"No," I said. "Our time was short, but I wouldn't give it up for anything."

We sat in silence for a moment or two, each of is lost in our own thoughts. If others in the room observed us, they might wonder about the two guys looking sadly reflective in the corner of the room.

I broke the silence. "Why did you get into law enforcement? I can see how it can be an exciting life on the one hand, and lonely on another. And dangerous too."

"Yeah. All of those things. Most people think Italians are usually on the other side of the law." He chuckled. "Don't tell me you never thought that. I know that's what a lot of people think."

"Martin Scorsese has seen to that."

"Anyway...I grew up poor in a tough neighborhood. My father was a hairdresser. I took a lot of grief because of that...bullying. Every day I heard I was a Wop...I was a Guinea. I kind of withdrew, pissed off at the world. I thought it wasn't fair. I joined the Army. Was an MP and liked it. Going into law enforcement was a natural next step. I guess after having been treated unfairly as a kid, the idea of justice had some appeal. So, here I am."

He broke into a broad smile. "An interesting part of the story. Over the years I've arrested two or three of the neighborhood kids who gave me a hard time. I'll never forget how they looked at me when I put on the cuffs. I wondered if they remembered the bullshit they pulled on me when we were kids. One of them asked me to let him go...for old times sake." e chortled. "I told him I was arresting him for old times sake."

"I'm sure you have a lot of stories to tell. You should write a book."

"I'm no John MacDonald. And I hate writing reports."

Nellie came by and asked if we wanted another round. Ansini and I looked at each other and nodded and away she went.

With fresh drinks on the table I took a deep breath. "Okay, it's been great going over our personal histories, but the reason we're here is because you said you might be able to help Mary Haller on the death certificate thing.

"This is a tough one. Lots of rules and regulations." He looked at me with a twinkle in his eye.

"So?..."

"In this state, it takes a body. If you have a body it's no big deal. It's automatic. In a missing persons case, it's a lot more complicated. There's a statute on the books. It requires a five year wait before a missing person can be presumed dead and a death certificate released."

"Seems like a long time."

"It is. Your insurance lobby at work."

"So, you're telling me it's a lost cause?"

"Not necessarily. I'm telling you friends in the right place can help."

"Ansini, I think you're baiting me."

"Yeah. Here's the deal." He looked in both directions. Satisfied that no one could hear him he went on. "Haller's a cold case. I've run it up the flagpole at the department and have asked if we have reached the point where we could presume Fred Haller to be dead. I think he is. We've done everything we could. The attorney said he would have no objection. It's a little fuzzy because of the state law, but he told me to go ahead and try. The department would like to close the case. This should do it."

He reached into his pocket and pulled out a letter. This is for Mary. It's the notification to her from the department's attorney that we now presume Fred Haller to be deceased." He handed it to me.

"Again, we're right on the line on this one. Virgin territory." He put his hands together as if in prayer.

"I have a friend in the County Vital Records Department. Hah...this is rich....turns out it's another one of those kids from the old neighborhood...one of the good ones. At least he is now." He rolled his eyes. "I had a chat with him and we worked something out."

"This is getting interesting. And?..."

"I convinced him that if I provided a statement saying Fred Haller is "presumed dead" by my department, he could issue a death certificate."

"Sounds illegal."

"Let's not use that word. Let's just say it's happening with a bit of a wink and a nod. I told him she's an old woman and a mess. I told him she's moving out of state and needs to get this thing re-solved. He's Italian...simpatico." He made the OK sign with his thumb and forefinger. "It comes naturally."

"A wink and a nod? A wink and a nod that could get you into trouble not to mention your buddy. The insurance company will squawk."

"Mary may have to hire a lawyer, but the department attorney...another friend of mine...thinks it'll fly. It's up to Mary." He locked his fingers. "Otherwise, it's four more years."

"So, what does she have to do?"

"Go to vital records and request the certificate. My friend says it's ready and waiting."

"Just like that?"

"Tell her to make a bunch of copies. She has to close out his life. It's like closing a bank account. She'll need copies for everything...insurance...Social Security...any joint accounts."

I gently slapped the letter into the palm of my hand. "Don't you want to give her the news? You've been working with her from the beginning."

"Trav, my friend. As of this moment, I'm out of it. I've done what I can. I think it'll work. But, I don't want my prints on it any more than they already are. Same with my friend."

I let the words sink in. The worst that could happen from Mary's point of view is that the insurance company would balk and she'd wind up having to wait another four years. She could say she requested the certificate because police had told her they considered her presumed dead and that the Vital Records folks granted the certificate.

"Ansini, why are you doing this for me...for Mary?"

"You're a good guy. Mary's good people."

He leaned back and thought for a moment. Maybe I think I owe you. "You kick started the investigation that could be very good for my career. AND...you introduced me to Travis McGee." The way he looked at me I couldn't really tell if he were joking or not, but I kind of thought he meant it.

"That's a good one. Just like you," I added, hoping I sounded as grateful as I was. "Thanks for everything."

"I gotta go." He stood to leave. "Thanks. And, by the way," he said sarcastically, "When is that article you said you were writing about me going to come out?"

It took me a second to remember our first meeting and my pretense for the meeting. I just shook my head. "Sorry about that." He was still laughing as he walked through the door on his way out.

When I told Mary she gasped and clutched her throat and had to sit down. She reread the department's letter. "This is so out of the blue. So unexpected." She stuttered..."I...I...I can't believe it." She shook her head. "My god...after all these months."

I went over the conversation I had had with Ansini and cautioned her to be sure that his name was not mentioned in connection with the matter. I, of course, had no idea about his contact at Vital Records. All I knew was that he was Italian and, as Ansini put it, "simpatico." I didn't want to know who it was. And, I wondered, what standing "simpatico" would have in any courtroom.

I explained to her that it was hardly a done deal and that she might have to go to the mat with the insurance people. It seemed to me, I told her, that she should hire an attorney when she filed her claim and perhaps have the lawyer do all the negotiating.

She wondered out loud if this was something she could do from out of state? I thought it would be best to hire locally, but that she didn't have to be here.

But the first step would be to actually have the death certificate in hand. For that she was on her own. I offered to go with her for moral support if she liked, but she said not to bother, that she felt she could handle it by herself.

"So you're going to go through with it?" I asked. "One hundred percent?"

"Of course. Why would I not?"

"Well, it seems to me there are some legal issues here. Maybe something could backfire. And, it occurs to me that Ansini and his friends could be in trouble if what they've done has crossed any lines. That could extend to you."

"Trav, as I see it, if the cops presume Fred dead, it's the most natural thing in the world for me to request the death certificate. Their position has to have some clout." I think she was getting a little miffed at my cautious attitude.

"Mary, you've got to know that the insurance company won't part with a buck if it can find an escape route. In this case, that may well be the law."

"I do have this letter. That has to have some weight. I think it could be open and shut. At least I hope so. If it has to go to the lawyers, Fred and I...I mean...I...can afford an attorney now." She appeared a little flustered. "Imagine that," she said, "After a year I still talk as if Fred were still here."

"I understand. I still talk to Holly."

There was an awkward silence before she spoke. "Trav, I can't thank you enough for all that you've done. I knew that if I contacted you about all of this, something good would happen. But I have to tell you I was thinking of you as a last resort."

"The last best hope?"

"Something like that."

"Well, I'm glad it seems to have worked out. I hope it's clear sailing ahead." I reached over and took her hands in mine. "I'm going to miss you."

"Me too."

I stood and admit to feeling a little emotional. I had known Mary Haller in years past, and her phone call brought us back into the same orbit. Now, she was leaving for a new life far away. "Time to go," I said.

"Thanks again so much Trav. I want to buy you the best dinner you ever had before I leave. I'll call you in a day or two. Lots going on...the house and all."

"I'm ready when you are." I could see her eyes moisten as mine were.

She came to me. We gave each other a big hug and I kissed her on the cheek. I left feeling pretty good about the way things had turned out, little knowing that I would never see her again.

MARY

Three months later, while the feds were still building their cases, and my friend Jeff continued to rebound, I received a letter from Mary Haller. She'd been gone for many weeks. I had expected a cheerful update about a new life in Florida. It was postmarked from Lillehammer, Norway.

Dear Trav: Surprise!

Time, finally, to give you a Haller update, to apologize for complicating your life, and for having been less than honest with you. I'm with Fred in Norway. I selfishly took advantage of you and complicated your life. I am truly sorry. You certainly deserve an apology.

Fact is I thought this would be an uncomplicated fraud. Fred and I decided some time ago that life was crap and that we were spinning our wheels in our final days. He wanted a new life...as a photographer believe it or not...and I was tired of the status quo. Snowbirds were flying south. We could not afford that...unless we won the lottery. For us the lottery was his insurance policy and some-place where that, and social security, could give us a good later life. We thought we had things so well planned.

Our big mistake was the insurance. We didn't realize it would be so difficult to collect. I should have known better. Insurance com-panies should have a tight fist on their logos.

We were thinking of sunshine and coco-nuts, but decided on the happy life, perma-frost, and socialized medicine. So, here we are in Norway. It's called the happiest country in the world. It is and we are. Happy that is.

And, the photographic world is magnifi-cent. Lillehammer is sensational. You might like to think about that too. Ever seen a fjord at sunrise or sunset? Or people who don't have the kind of social worries in what I now call "the old country?" You aren't getting any younger you know. Hah!!

You deserve to know the story.

You have no idea how I rehearsed before calling you. It had to be good. You've been around too long and have seen and heard too much BS to be fooled easily. I surprised my-self at how easily I was able to deceive. I even managed a tear from time to time. It was all easier because you are so trusting of friends. And, frankly, I was counting on your thinking kindly of me for my supporting you when that little bitch turned on you. Now, you have been victimized again. This time by an admirer. I cannot tell you how guilty I feel about that. But Fred has always been my North Star. In this case, literally.

Fred was here in Norway all along. I visited twice. Everyone thought I was with friends in Florida and off on a river cruise. More deceit. As I write this I realize that I have not been a very good person throughout the charade.

All Fred took with him when he left was a wallet full of phony identification, his camera and a new lust for life. I fibbed when I said I didn't know what he did with the camera. One of many fibs. I'll call them fibs. You may choose another word and I wouldn't blame you.

Once he was gone, I missed him more and more with every passing day. Although I knew he was alive and well, it was like I was in mourning because he was not with me. At times I felt as if he really were dead.

You may remember he was an official with the glazier's union. Although he worked with his hands and his back, he also had a very good mind. He had access to the person-

nel records and personal information of union members. He used his union position to acquire enough personal information about two or three dead members to create a new identity. He got a passport, new credit cards, new everything. Leaving his wallet and old identity behind was a nice touch I thought. We actually had fun working it all out.

And it worked out well for a lot of reasons. One was that it gave us something else to think about. For the first time in our marriage, we had found ourselves getting on each other's nerves when he retired. He was home too much. My routine was totally upended. Remember, I retired first, so my days were pretty much set. He struggled with finding ways to spend his time. He was not a reader nor a man with many interests. Until he bought that camera. Before that we were bickering over little things...lots of little things. I was bothered that he watched too much television during the day. He was annoyed when I had to ask him to lift his feet when I vacuumed the living room. Things as inconsequential as that. I nagged. He was embarrassed.

We felt a lifetime loving relationship slipping away. He eventually took up photography as a hobby and really took to it. It got him out of the house. There were so many *opportunities and subjects to shoot around town. He was excited and alive again, and that invigorated me. He began to daydream. So did I. We began saying things like "what if?" So we hatched our plot. I hate putting it like that. But...*

He is thriving. This is such a beautiful country and he seems fully determined to photograph every square inch. He's thinking about a book showing his best work. So, if you ever see a book of Norwegian landscape photographs shot by a deceased glazier, you'll know who it was.

I have to say that the night we all had dinner you almost threw me for a loop when you asked about the photography books. I had just sent them to Fred that afternoon. He'd been clamoring for them.

I am keeping busy teaching English as a second language in the local elementary school. Easy work. Most of the kids speak English better than I do.

Again, I apologize. I've always known you to be a compassionate soul and I thought if I took advantage of that and got you involved, you could find a way to get that death certificate to me a lot faster than otherwise. And, of course, you did. Indirectly, but you did. Thanks for that. And thanks to Detective Ansini. I'd love to give him a hug. I'm not so sure he'd hug back.

I am still haggling with the insurance company. It's complicated. Apparently there are insurance companies who have insurance companies, and some of them are offshore. It's like a Russian egg...or an onion. You open or peel one level and it leads to another. Let's hope there's no dead end. But my attorney is confident that we'll outlast them. When, or if, that happens, we'll be able to live very well here. You can by a lot of Krone with U.S. dollars. The standard of living is very high. No property taxes. People live well into their eighties. If we make eighty, it will have all been worth it. Life is good!

I had to do some fast thinking a couple of times with you. Remember when I slipped and talked about Fred and me hiring an attorney? That was a big oops, but I apparently recovered well. I did didn't I?

And I think I did a pretty good acting job on your DNA visit. I didn't think I had it in me. It was easier knowing he was alive and that no DNA was going to prove he was dead.

Jenny was an interesting experience. You would not believe what she was willing to buy my house for if it didn't sell. I had the feeling she would not work very hard to sell it. So, that worked out okay. We are happy to no longer have to look out over that hideous gar-

den of theirs.

I'm almost sorry I killed her dog. I did get tired of it pooping on my lawn and Jenny never cleaning it up. And they had the nerve to write their nasty notes about our yard. I guess it was good enough for Dolly or Daisy or whatever its name was to crap in. Who they hell did they think they were?

That, and both of them maligning me and my dear Fred by thinking he'd run away from me, or that I had killed him and that he was lying dead in the basement. What an obnoxious couple. When I told her I was not going to sign a contract with her on the house I truly felt that she would find a way to do me harm. Sorry she was killed in that car of hers. I promise I had nothing to do with it. Hah! So far no tears.

That brings me to Jeff. I hope he is on the mend. If you choose to tell anyone about my deceit please tell him he is in my thoughts and prayers. I will leave the decision as to whom, or whether to tell, to you.

Finally, I guess no crime goes unpunished. There is some news that is not happy even in this happy place. I have been diagnosed with breast cancer. It remains to be seen how serious. I think I could use a prayer. What a disappointment it would be if, after our glorious con...our deceit, if it all came tum-

bling down. The doctors here are wonderful. Don't let anyone tell you socialized medicine isn't a wonderful thing. Taxes are high but worth it.

My dear friend...if you ever have a hankering to see the fjords, give me a buzz. I'd love to see you and give you a big, apologetic kiss. If you'd prefer to have nothing ever to do with me, I understand. But, there is always an open invitation.

I'm really not a selfish person, except when I am.

I'm sorry! I'm sorry! I'm sorry!

Thank you. Thank you. Thank you!

Affectionately, Mary.

PS: Fred sends his best.

I still don't know whether I've been played or have simply been a character in someone else's play. Her story is remarkable on all counts. I admire and respect the devotion she and Fred obviously have for each other. I can only appreciate and understand their desire to spend their final days together and be able to do so in relative financial security. I would have chosen a warmer climate, but that's just me.

No one likes to feel manipulated, but I have to give them both high marks for pulling it off and for their patience and creativity. They risked a lot. Had she not sold the house, and if they had to wait four more years for the insurance money, who knows how it might have played out.

I don't feel like a victim. More like a chess piece in a complicated game that I will call a draw. If there is a victim in all of this I guess it's the insurance company. Maybe I should say "potential victim." But it's hard to work up much sympathy for it. It still hasn't given up a single dollar and it would have paid off one day anyway.

Should I bring this letter from Mary to Ansini and let him in on the gag? I thought about that and wrestled with all the options. The answer? No. He might not respond well. Let him continue to think that what he did was right and compassionate. After all, it was.

I asked myself what would Travis McGee do?

I took the letter, crumpled it in both hands, and tossed it into the trash I raised my glass high. Boodles of course. "Well done Mary Haller. Well done. And of course, I will pray for you."

MCGEE'S EPILOG

Life went on, for me and for some of the people I had come to know. Over the course of the following weeks and months I was able to keep track of some of the people I had come to know and know about.

Detective Ansini and I had become friends. We continue to see each other from time to time and compare notes on Travis McGee. I was delighted when he was given a big promotion. It would ensure much more prosperous retirement.

DeNeisha Trotter was on her way. She was appointed to an important Assistant Attorney General position with the U.S. Department of Justice. So much for becoming the State Attorney General. Who knows where the appointment would take her on the national level. My money's on her going a long, long way.

The DEA and FBI announced some arrests in connection with opioid trafficking that had brought such large quantities of the drug to this and other states. A drug compounding operation outstate was shut down. They were working with the government of Mexico to indict several men and women who had been involved in supplying American distributors in our state and others. The name Angel kept coming up.

Gary Goodstrich was recovering from a near fatal beating in federal prison where he was serving the minimum sentence on drug distribution and related charges.

I ran into Troy Hacker while he was walking his dog. I remembered he was not fond of dogs, but he told me he finally decided to get one to help keep rabbits and other critters out of the "Back 40." He calls the dog "Jenny."

Jeff Carr is on the mend, but it has not been an easy time for him. His age has slowed things down. The recovery process has been long, often painful and required another surgery. I stayed with him when he came home from the hospital for few days until his son Bill arranged for some in-home care. We get together to play backgammon when he feels he's able.

Andy, I learned, was Nellie's father. He owned the place.

I have no idea about Mary. She has not written. I have no address for her. I don't know if she is alive or dead. I hope she's enjoying the fruits of her "con" as she called it.

For me the adventure is over. On reflection, do I feel betrayed? Do I feel played? Yes to both questions. But I understand.

Bottom line...grab a little of what's left and hope for the best. Long live Mary and Fred. And if I may, the same to me.

ABOUT THE AUTHOR

Don Marsh

Marsh is a retired award winning broadcast journalist. He is the author of three published works of non-fiction.
*Flash Frames...Journey of a Journeyman Journalist
*How to be Rude Politely
*Coming of Age...Liver Spots and All
A Wink and a Nod is his first work of fiction
He lives in St. Louis

Made in the USA
Monee, IL
16 March 2023

29992213R00144